ORBIT

ORBIT
Life with My People

Orbit

ORBIT
LIFE WITH MY PEOPLE

iUniverse books may be ordered through booksellers or by contacting:

iUniverse
1663 Liberty Drive
Bloomington, IN 47403
www.iuniverse.com
1-800-Authors (1-800-288-4677)

ISBN: 978-1-4917-6305-6 (sc)
ISBN: 978-1-4917-6304-9 (e)

Library of Congress Control Number: 2015905037

Print information available on the last page.

iUniverse rev. date: 04/11/2015

Dedicated
to
My beloved Bettine
and All my People

CONTENTS

"Orbit is not just a dog; he's a spiritual being…"

Yakov Smirnoff

PROLOGUE

PETER DROPPED DOWN BESIDE ME with a piece of paper in his hand. "Listen, Orby," he said, "this is a letter for you from Bettine." He started to read, and I could tell it was a passionate letter about my life. At points, Peter even laughed as he read. Then he came to this part, and he looked deeply into my eyes:

"I thank you with all my heart for being in my life so long—now nearly sixteen years! You are the star of my life and being, and in every show I play now and forevermore, you are the biggest star, because in my multi-media show from screen and stage you spread your love to millions all over the world. When you go into the other worlds and over the Rainbow Bridge, know that we will always celebrate your continuing presence and life on earth—you were the best thing that came out of that community adventure."

Momentarily, I thought of the children's song at the Unity church: "We are walking in the light, in the light, in the light; we are walking in the light, in the light of God." *I wonder what it will really be like in these other worlds and over the Rainbow Bridge?*

Peter paused in the reading, as if he knew I was in thought. He patted me on my head to bring back my attention.

"There was a lot of hardship," he continued. "But all the losses and sufferings were worth it just for you." Peter started to choke up, before continuing to read Bettine's words. "I love you, Orby, with all my heart! I shall miss you, but you will always be in my heart wherever I go, and you will never be forgotten by any being you have known. If a new dog comes into my life, he'll bring me *your* presence. It's all love. All else is illusion. I love you forever, your human mother, Bettine."

I could tell from Peter's eyes that he was thinking something, and

I just instinctively knew what. I remembered those two portraits of that dog by the front door at Alpha Meadows. I knew this dog was special to Peter from some time in his life. I had even heard him speak to the drawings. All he said was, "I love you, Woolly..." He didn't say "I loved you." It was as if for him, Woolly was forever. *Could Woolly also be me?* I put forward my paw and tapped Peter's wrist as he lay beside me.

A few days later, on a morning when I found it particularly hard to stand up, Peter pressed his phone to my ear. I heard Bettine's voice... "Orby, you're such a good doggie...such a good doggie." Then the sound of her flute filled my ears.

"That was Bettine, wasn't it?" Marie said.

"Yes, she played her flute for Orby, one more time."

I knew. We dogs do know. Perhaps humans know, too? *Finality, I know it. My legs have got so much worse. I've fallen many times.* Peter and Marie tried to hold me up, but again I collapsed. They guided me to the rug. I liked it there, and I lay down. I was comfortable, but I couldn't walk.

"Are you thinking what I'm thinking?" Peter said.

"Yes," Marie replied.

Finality. Now I was certain. *Have I made a difference in their lives... the lives of all those humans that I came to know? Did they see my light?*

Later, with Peter and Marie holding up my hips, I stumbled out onto the lawn. I sat on the grass in the sun, just as I always had on the oval lawn at Alpha Meadows. It was a beautiful spring day. Marie groomed me, gently caressing my coat with my favorite brush. Peter lay on the grass beside me, looking into my eyes. He held my paw. *I know. It's all right. I know.*

They lifted me into the car. It was only a short drive. They carried me out and set me down in this veterinary office. It was not Dr. Espey's place, but it smelled the same. A chocolate-colored dog came in—a Labrador. He came over to play. He must have been a puppy. I put out my paw for him. I tried to get up, but I couldn't. Two nice girls came out to talk to me. They took us into a private place and then left. For a long time, Marie groomed me, while I sat with Peter. I could see his eyes were moist. He was stroking me under my chin. *It's all right. It's all right. I'm over fifteen years old. I've had a wonderful life.* At length, the girls came back. They shaved a patch on my back foot, and there was a prick as a needle went in. *Did I accomplish my goal? Did I spread the light to my humans?* I felt at peace as I continued to look at Peter, then the room went fuzzy. In an instant, I saw...felt...smelled...and breathed my whole life....

CHAPTER ONE

A Log Cabin in the Ozarks

"I simply run, play, and explore every day."

THE DOOR TO JOHNNY'S LOG cabin was open. Mama told us that we could hear the river. We cocked our keen ears. Over the stillness of the winter landscape came a babbling sound.

"What's the river?" I asked.

"A place where water rushes over pebbles and cuts into rocks below bluffs, where fish swim, where wild flowers grow. It flows through gorges, feeds into caves that echo. One day, Johnny will take us there."

I nuzzled into Mama's warm white fur to feed, jostled by my brothers and sisters.

We never knew which of us was the oldest. Mama just said, "You were all born at the same time." I believe it was in January of '98.

Johnny came back in with a couple of logs from the woodpile. He fed the kitchen stove, before sitting back in his rocking chair. On the kitchen floor was a worn rug covering random-width boards. Mama liked to lie on it close to the stove, while we all snuggled up to her. Johnny, whose blue eyes twinkled set below crooked brows that were graying like his hair, called Mama, Precious. He wasn't very tall, but robust, with large laboring hands. Something about him was almost elf-like. Funny creatures, elves, but I will tell you about them later. Reaching down, Johnny picked me up. My legs went swimming in the air. We rubbed noses. I could smell him, a comforting musky odor, and I could feel his love.

We didn't leave the warm kitchen, although from time to time people came to visit. We shared the room with a cat, which seemed almost always to be asleep. If we got too close, we became wary of the animal, and sometimes, she would open one eye and glare at us, so we usually gave her a wide berth. Johnny never seemed to call the cat anything other than, Kitty, so we presumed that to be her name.

One day, when the door opened, it was very bright outside. Everything looked white. A woman with a round face came in, accompanied by a tall man with a beard and sparkling eyes. They stomped their boots. Johnny got up from his chair, still holding me in his big hands. I looked up at the woman. She had a beautiful smile.

"This is the runt," Johnny said. "He's my favorite."

My tail wagged.

"Oh, how precious!" the lady said. She looked at her partner, "Brian, how absolutely precious!"

Mama raised her eyes to look at this woman.

Johnny laughed. "She thinks you're calling her," he said, handing me to the lady. "That's her name...Precious."

The lady laughed, too. "This little one's like a snowball."

"That was quite a snowfall," Johnny said, walking away to feed another log into the stove. He started to boil a kettle. Soon, the warmth of the log cabin drew vapor out of the visitors' wet clothes, causing a fuggy aroma. The kettle whistled, adding steam to the mix. Johnny poured boiling water into mugs and dropped little bags on a string into each. "How's Billy?" he asked.

"They love it here," the lady replied. "As soon as the snow is gone, do you think you could plow the bottom land? Then we'll start preparing the gardens. We need to get the potatoes started."

"I'll get down there as soon as I can."

"Joanne's friends are going to help us with the gardens," Brian added.

Oh...so this is Joanne. I licked her cheek.

Joanne smiled. "Yes, Donnie and Kate from Strafford. They're quite the gardeners," she continued, before she let me down, and I scampered back to Mama and my brothers and sisters. Nurtured by Mama's milk, I felt sleepy by the time Joanne and Brian left.

Eventually, when spring came, Johnny moved us out into a pen attached to a large doghouse. We rarely used the doghouse. By now, my brothers, sisters, and I, were pretty active, and we were beginning to bark. We could hear birds chirping in the foliage of the trees, and yes… we could hear the river.

"Mama says it's called the Finley," one of my brothers told me, "a river that flows through the Ozarks. She says we'll be able to visit there soon, when Johnny goes fishing."

We were scampering around in the spring sun, when the day came, and Johnny let us out of the pen. We followed him and Mama down the gravel road, into the valley, and to a bridge over the river. Below the bridge, I walked toward the wet pebbles and took my first tentative step into water. It was cold and it felt strange. I jumped, shook my paw, and ran back to the grass. *My paws, they're getting so big.*

"Mama says we'll grow into them," my brother informed me. "One day, we'll be big."

"Who was our daddy?" I asked.

"Mama never says," answered my brother, cocking his head to one side and raising his ears. "I've asked her, but she doesn't really know. Somebody with a big white dog came to see Johnny. Like Mama, this dog was apparently a Great Pyrenees…that's what we are…Great Pyrenees."

"So, we'll be as big as Mama?"

"I suppose that's why they call us Great?"

"And what are Pyrenees?"

"Mama says they're mountains in Spain."

"Spain?"

"A place where they speak Spanish…a long way from here."

"Wow! It sounds like we were once a pretty big deal."

"We herded sheep, but there are not too many sheep here in the Ozarks. I guess now we just take care of people. But Mama told me we once pulled carts in a terrible war across the ocean."

"What's a war?"

"Fierce barking!"

"And…the ocean?"

"Yeah…a place where rivers take their water…a long way from here."

"How do you know so much?"

"Oh, I listen to Johnny when he talks to Mama."

Mama came to us and shook her whole body. Water sprayed over us. Then we sat and felt the warmth of the sun. We could hear the rush of the water, and see white clouds scurrying overhead. Johnny caught a fish. "Cat-fish," he said. "I'll cook it tonight." Mama looked up at him and twitched her nose. We could smell an oily odor, which mingled with a scent of earthiness. It was an ugly fish, and I could see why they called it a cat-fish. It had long whiskers, just like Kitty.

With the fish in a canvas bag, Johnny walked us back up the hill to our log cabin. We could see the kitchen stovepipe emitting rings of wood-smoke. And there were our pen and the big doghouse. Grass was growing all around, along with dandelions and daisies. Skeletons of rusting machinery…a sidebar mower, an old truck, a log-splitter, car doors, rubber tires, and a large tractor with a blade in front…this was Johnny's world, and it was now our world. Some outbuildings and a rail fence separated our patch from a neighbor's field, where occasionally cattle roamed.

Later in the summer, someone came to the house and looked us over. Johnny picked up my brother and handed him to the stranger. Pieces of paper were exchanged. My brother was gone. *I miss him. My brother was wise. He taught me many things that he learned from Mama.* Then someone else came for one of my sisters.

"Will we all go?" I asked Mama.

"Probably…we don't usually stay together."

That's sad. I wonder where they are now? But just like my brother said, "We take care of people." *That's what we do now.*

The day came when Johnny picked me up out of the pen. He wrapped me in a blanket and put me in a basket. I let out a squeaky bark in protest. Johnny smiled at me, while stroking my head. He placed the basket beside him in his old truck, and started the noisy motor. I looked back at the pen, where the residue of our family had their paws up on the wire netting. They were barking. The truck started to move. Johnny drove it out onto the road, and we crossed the bridge over the river. We passed fields with blue wildflowers and buttercups…a trailer or two parked a little ways from the gravel road…cows and horses. Eventually, we turned onto a rough road, and went up a steep hill. The road wound its way through leafy oaks and spasmodic cedars until it came out in a clearing with great views. We stopped, and Johnny picked me up and took me to a cabin set partly in the hillside and partly on stilts. There, we were greeted by the lady with the round face…Joanne Green.

Johnny handed me over to her, and I nestled in her arms.

"For you," he said. "I want you to have my favorite, before he gets taken by someone else."

"Really?" she said joyfully. "He's so special…a little bundle of fluff."

Johnny looked up at Joanne, "Yes," he said, "but look at the size of his feet…he'll grow into them. He'll be a big dog, just like Precious."

Johnny left, but looked back and waved. I gave out a little bark, and then looked up into Joanne's face. I licked it. It seemed I had a new home.

CHAPTER TWO

Community Dog

"Why does everything smell so good?"

MOST OF JOANNE'S COMMUNITY CABIN was taken up by a large bed. There was also a table, piled with papers and about half-a-dozen coffee mugs. A ladder led up into a loft, and below this loft, windows looked out on that spectacular view over the hills around our Finley valley. A bookcase held a few tattered volumes, and there were two or three assorted kitchen chairs. People came in and out all the time…the men, with long, unkempt hair, and stubbly chins. *These are my new people?* The women were cooking pungent greens and lots of beans in a little kitchen off the main room; and they were always making coffee and tea, the coffee having a strong aroma, purveying fug and warmth that drifted through the cabin. The kitchen was usually full of steam.

Outside the cabin, were two picnic tables, and in the evening, the people came together to eat their rice, beans, and vegetables. It was there, this first summer evening, I met Rajah. Although he was a small, terrier-like dog, he was larger than I was. He barked ferociously when he saw me. He called me, Powder Puff. I wasn't sure I liked him, but I could see that he was devoted to Joanne's companion, Brian Hadwick, the man who seemed to be in charge. I remembered him from that visit they made to Johnny's cabin in the snow. Oh, that first night, how I missed Johnny and Mama.

At first, I stayed close to Joanne. She was kind to me, and she called me, Fluff. With her, I began to discover my new territory that Joanne called, Sarvis Point. There seemed no bounds. Trails and pathways led off into woods of oaks and cedars, with clearings here and there where little cabins could be found. A family lived in one. They had a small child, whom they called, Gabriel. The boy's mother had a weird name; it sounded like Maryloulena, and the man she lived with was Leone. Sometimes, they just called each other Lou and Leo. *Lou and Leo, I suppose they kind of fit together.*

Often, we went down to the vegetable gardens below our cabin and near the road. Joanne used to wear a big straw hat when she gardened, and there was always laughter among those working in this area. I met Kate and Donnie. Kate wore a hat just like Joanne's—a jolly woman. Sometimes, another woman also worked in the garden. I remember a day when she had her son with her—a husky boy.

"He's growing," Kate said.

"Taylor or the pup?" Joanne asked.

Taylor rolled his eyes.

I looked down at my paws. *I'll be growing a lot more than this. Of course I'm growing! I'll be as big as Mama!*

But as I grew, the humans never seemed to get any bigger, except perhaps Gabriel.

I liked the gardens. There were rows of potatoes, carrots, lettuces, peas, kale, and cabbages. Squash and tomatoes clung to wire frames, and there were several sorts of peppers. I learned these plants' names from listening to Joanne and Kate. Brian was often down there, too, but he seemed mostly interested in digging holes; so I started digging with my paws.

"Get out of there!" Maryloulena yelled.

I looked up, startled.

"You're digging up the carrots, you stupid dog!"

Joanne laughed. "Fluff, no digging," she said.

I glanced back at Maryloulena, then walked over to Joanne and nuzzled her.

"We love you, Fluff, just don't dig up the carrots," she repeated.

I became wary of Maryloulena.

In a clearing in the woods, lived Clive. He had a cat that I chased, which didn't please Clive, but like Joanne, Clive was kind to me. Dick, too, lived in the woods. He seemed a little different from the others, and also often worked in the vegetable gardens. Clive and Dick both sometimes shared their food with me. Joanne gave me the same food that Rajah enjoyed, but I was wary of getting too close to Rajah's dish. In fact, in time, I got much of my food from those scraps at the communal table.

At Johnny's, because we lived mostly in the pen, our family were always very clean, but here, I soon got dirty. I used to run around in the woods, and find exciting things that stank—deer carcasses, dead armadillos, and the like. I got into one of these dead armadillos, and when I returned to the communal supper I promptly threw up. From then on, most these people called me, Chucky.

Late that summer, a friend of Brian's joined us. He was an Australian, whatever that means—he had a funny accent, but he was nice to me. He, too, had a weird name—Arlo. He worked a lot with Brian, tearing out brush, digging holes, and planting trees. With Clive and Brian, he started working on an old silo tower in one of the bottom meadows. They poured concrete, and started to erect steel pillars and beams. Arlo laughed when I peed on the steel beams that were waiting to be attached to the pillars. "Orbit! Show some respect," he said. "This is going to be our community pavilion."

Summer turned to fall, and the trees in the woods became a glorious riot of golden colors. Leaves fell, and smelled earthy and interesting as they carpeted the ground. Community meals moved inside. The cabin filled up with cooking odors. Windows steamed up. It was warm in the cabin. I liked the fug, but I still kept my distance from Rajah. I don't think he would have ever let me on the bed.

Sometimes, after the meal, Joanne and Brian had everyone participate in a certain exercise. They started loud, with everyone talking at once as they sat opposite each other, and then it got quieter. But after the exercise, I felt that these community people suddenly started to glow and look serene. *Strange.* When it got completely quiet, I'd fall asleep.

Winter was boring, until the white flakes fell again, and our hillside became a place where I could slide and play. Community members slid down the hills, sitting on big trashcan lids. Like Johnny, they called the white stuff, snow. There was much laughter when Leone's lid spun round and crashed into Dick's, toppling Dick off so he rolled down the hill. I barked fiercely at Leone, but he just laughed. "It's all right, Chucky, it's only fun." I loved the snow, too. By now, I had such a thick coat of white fur that I never felt cold, and I was almost as big as Mama.

Almost as quickly as the snow came, so it went away, and little green leaves started to come out again. At first, they were just in the undergrowth of the woods, but later, the tall trees the people called, oaks, broke into foliage, and the sun started to feel warm again. This was a feverish time of work down in the gardens. We were now going to have large asparagus beds. Everybody seemed excited about that, and the garden area nearly doubled.

Three ladies came to the communal supper one evening, again with strange names—Holly, Bernadette, and a red-head named Sonja. They'd spent the afternoon with Joanne and Brian, looking at neighboring land, and I'd gone with them, along with Rajah and their dog, Trail. It was just north of our woods, and there was a pond beside an old shed where Holly said they'd build their "stables." *Funny word?* I immediately liked Trail, a German Shepherd, and I followed him into the pond. The water felt cool and refreshing. When we came out, we shook ourselves just like Mama, but Bernadette got wet.

"No, Chucky!" she yelled.

"Trail!" Holly echoed.

Trail looked at me with knowing eyes.

About two thirds up the hill was an area with a view across the valley to our woods. Bernadette and Holly talked to each other excitedly before agreeing with Brian that this would be where they'd build.

"It's perfect for a berm house," Brian said, "exactly in keeping with what we're trying to do."

Holly nodded in agreement, and I sat down with Trail.

"So, we might be neighbors?" Trail suggested. "This might be my kingdom." *My kingdom? I'd like to have my own kingdom.*

Holly and Brian shook hands. Joanne talked earnestly with Sonja. They had struck some kind of a deal. Trail looked up at them, quizzically.

A week or two later, men came and bulldozed a road up to the site of the berm house. I watched with Trail. Arlo and Brian started to build fences. During this time, Holly, Bernadette, and Trail, also spent many evenings with us at the cabin, and Trail would get into trouble if he tried to steal any of the food. They didn't pay much attention to me, however, and from time to time, I cleaned off their plates.

Another afternoon, I went with Joanne, Brian, and Sonja, up above the area where Holly's berm house was being built. Brian had some kind of a wheel and tape, and with Sonja, he hammered stakes into a big pasture on the top of the hill. A roadway had already been bulldozed along the ridge, and the stakes marked eight divisions within the field, where grass, and orange and white wild flowers, grew taller than me. Some of them smelled sweet, and others sour. Sonja was writing on a board. "This works perfectly," she said. "The lots are all close to five acres."

"Now, the people will come," Brian said. "We'll be a new Findhorn." *What's a Findhorn?*

I wandered off into the tall grasses until I found a pond—a large pond right on the top of the hill. "It must be spring fed," Brian said. I lifted my leg on a tree, then waded into the water and cooled off.

The next week, most my people went away. Clive stayed and fed me. I was left to roam about the hills of our land. I noticed how quickly weeds started to grow in the vegetable gardens. Like the others, Clive continued to call me, Chucky. Johnny came to visit. I was pleased to see him. He smelled good, in fact, I smelled Mama. Johnny hadn't forgotten me. He rubbed my ears in that way I always liked, and he told me Mama and my remaining brother and sister were fine. *I wonder if I'll ever see them again?* Then late on a long summer evening, the big van came back with the community members. They were laughing and happy and they all had that serene look.

Not long after, many more visitors arrived. Some camped in tents down by our river—the Little Finley. There was a swimming hole near the campground, and the people swam there, naked. Others shared our cabins. I liked the company, and after their community meal, I used to walk with the new people through the woods, escorting them to their cabins. *This is my task...to help the humans.* They could easily see my white fur in the semi-dark.

In late summer, two unusual people came to visit. One had a voice a bit like Arlo the Australian, but more clipped and refined. They both dressed rather well, in contrast to most of my people, who were very casual in dress. The lady had blonde hair, expressive eyes, sparkles on her face, and seemed always to be carrying some sort of a pipe. At the communal meal, she played music on the pipe, and also tried to play for me and Rajah. "The magic flute," Joanne called it. And the sounds of the notes did seem magic as they rose up from our hillside. I cocked my somewhat muddy ears, and listened. The music made me drool and slobber, and that didn't please the gentleman. Several times, while the lady was playing, I saw opportunity to put my paws up on the picnic table and catch the remnants on plates with my tongue. Arlo tried to shoo me away. The lady stopped playing the music. "What's his name?" she asked.

"Chucky," Arlo said.

The music started again. Rajah sat in Brian's arms and stared at the lady, enraptured by the sounds. My people were also spellbound by the music, and I must say, I'd never heard anything like it myself. It greatly enhanced my sense of color, especially the high notes. I mostly saw only dull colors—grays, browns, blues, and odd splashes of pink— but in this music, I started to see much brighter colors—yellows, reds, orange, green, and even purple.

When darkness came, the night sky became pitch black, and the stars bright as the crystals in snowflakes. The lady looked up. "How beautiful," she said. "I don't think I've ever seen stars like that. I never thought too much about those stars. They were always there at night—a canopy of pinpricks in the sky. Johnny had told us that they were angels, watching over us. *So many angels! We watch over the humans and the angels watch over us all. Maybe?*

At length, the visitors drove away as they weren't staying in our cabins or camping. I heard that they were staying with friends of Joanne and Brian at an inn not too far away. "We'll show them the lots at eleven," Brian said to Sonja. "They'll be the next to build—many will follow."

The next morning, the shiny red vehicle the visitors drove pulled up our drive between the oaks and cedars. I ran down the hill to meet it. "That dog," I heard the man say, "that dreadful slobbering dog…that's just one thing that makes me doubt this venture, that dog and that kid with the naked backside." *Gabriel. Yes, he's always half-naked, but are they talking about me…a dreadful slobbering dog?*

It was a beautiful day, the clouds creating moving shadows across our Ozark hills. The visitors, who had the names of Bettine and Peter, went off with Joanne, Brian, and Sonja. I wasn't invited. I sat down outside the cabin and looked out over our land. I could hear Maryloulena calling to Gabriel down in the vegetable gardens. Kate was down there, too. Maryloulena and Kate were harvesting as much as they could for canning.

There was excitement at the evening meal when Bettine and Peter joined us. "Congratulations!" Brian said.

"Two teddy bears sitting in the field marked the spot!" Sonja exclaimed.

Joanne laughed.

What's going on? It sounds like these people might be coming to live with us.

Meanwhile, Maryloulena prattled on about the importance of the canning. "We must be self-sufficient when the millenium comes." *Millenium? What's that?* I sniffed around Peter's feet. Then Bettine started to play music on one of her wooden pipes that I now had learned are flutes. She came close to me. *She's playing for me. I like these people.*

The next day, I followed Brian and Rajah as they drove our yellow backhoe up the hill, passing where builders were finishing work on Holly's and Bernadette's house. Trail wasn't there, but Clive was still working on the fences. When the backhoe reached the big cow pasture with its pond, it turned left and down to a rather stony area. I watched from a distance. I was afraid of this big, yellow monster of a machine. Brian started to dig into the hillside. Rajah barked at the bucket. I could have joined him, but I wasn't quite sure what was going on. *Is this the Findhorn?* I sat down, my eyes glued to the moving machine, but eventually as I lay with my head on my paws close to the ground, I became aware of the buzz of insects. The sound of insects was very strong in our hills. Momentarily, my gaze became distracted as I thought I saw little things moving in the grass. I thought of Maryloulena, who was always going on about ticks. *What are ticks? Little insects?*

That evening, I found out. Joanne squeezed a small tube of liquid into my fur just behind my head, where I couldn't lick at it. Rajah got the same treatment. "For the ticks," she said. "We can't let you have ticks, Chucky." *Yes, but what are they?*

Maryloulena squealed, "Leo...quick. I have a tick!"

Leone twisted his thumb and forefinger on a little black spot on her shoulder. "Bloodsuckers!" he said.

Bloodsuckers? I ran into the meadow and rolled around. I loved this time of the day, bloodsuckers or no bloodsuckers. The sun was setting to the west, and the whole meadow was now alive with a deafening sound—a chorus of crickets, grasshoppers, and cicadas, interspersed with the high-pitched notes of little, green tree frogs. The sound of the frogs made the sky change for me into beautiful colors before darkness came.

CHAPTER THREE

The House on the Hill

"I like to hold my head up and feel the wind ruffle my face."

JOANNE AND BRIAN MOVED INTO a trailer across the road and not far from the gardens. Her son, Job, joined them. Without the bed in the community cabin, we all had more room. Holly and Bernadette then moved into their house up the road, and Trail and I became firm friends. Not long after, work started on another house in the meadow above Trail's place. Trail and I thought we should investigate it. Bulldozers and diggers had gouged a level platform out of the hill, forming a vast area of shale and stones. Trucks were busy offloading gravel to form a roadway. Brian was busy with the backhoe, digging trenches. Rajah barked at us as if this was *his* property. "I don't think we're welcome here," Trail said. "Let's go back in the woods."

I followed my friend. Even though it was early October, the day was warm, and the woods were cool. The forest floor crackled beneath our feet. Then a strong, rotten smell suggested to us a deer carcass was near. Trail found it, and we tugged at it. There was very little flesh left, and ants oozed out from the remains. It proved rather disappointing, so we let it go.

The next time we ventured up to the house on the hill, the roadway was completed, and piles of timber and shelf-rock lay scattered about the building site. Rajah was not there, so we sniffed around. "Funny smell," I said, checking out the timber.

"Treated," Trail informed me. "It was the same at our house."

We approached one of the pallets of shelf-rock. After I had peed on one corner, Trail added his claim to the pallet, and we went on down into the gouged-out hillside. While we were inspecting trenches and plastic pipes, I saw a rabbit running. I chased after it, but it escaped in the tall fescue. Trail still seemed to be laying claim to more of those pallets. "Let's go home," I barked. Trail looked up, sniffed the air, and bounded toward me. We ran all the way down Holly's and Bernadette's hill to the vegetable gardens. Maryloulena and Joanne were busy picking beans and squash. The clunking sound of Brian digging with the backhoe drifted on the air.

Our curiosity remained, and Trail and I visited the site up on the hill many times. A tall windmill now stood there that Brian looked on with pride, his hands on his hips. After we laid claim to the windmill, we followed a long trench leading to the building site. A large, concrete platform now covered the area where those pipes had protruded. The pipes looked like they were stuck in the concrete. We peed on them, too. On two sides of the platform, heavy abutment walls held back the raw earth. More piles of timber lay around, and one day, while we were there, a van drove up with all these people. They didn't look like ordinary people. They had weather-beaten faces and long, curly, dark hair. Their blue shirts looked coarse. Big suspenders held up their dark trousers. Most of them wore black, round-brimmed hats. The man in charge, however, was more like our people—a man with graying hair and normal clothing. He was carrying scrolls of paper that he opened up on top of one of the pallets of shelf-rock. The men looked over them, speaking to each other in a strange language. I went over and sniffed at their trousers. They smelled different. One of them kicked me out of the way. I growled. *I'm not sure I like these people.* I scampered back to Trail. "There's just something strange about those people," I said.

"They stink like rotting deer," Trail answered. "Humans are not supposed to smell like deer." He started to bark at them, so I barked, too. *I don't think they like dogs.*

Other trucks arrived with even more timber, and in time, the strange-looking men started to cut the wood with a big circular machine that made a high-pitched noise that sounded scary. We kept our distance, but watched. Later that day, Brian and Rajah drove up with Peter—the man with that funny accent, who'd visited us with the lady who plays the flutes. Brian introduced Peter to the man in charge. "Meet Steve Owens," he said, and then he talked to the other men, sometimes using sentences that sounded strange like the way they talked among themselves. He seemed to know them. Several times, I heard the name, "Schwartz."

"So, who are they?" I asked Trail.

"Builders," Trail replied. "Carpenters."

"Why do they smell different?"

"I think they're Amish," Trail replied. "Holly talks about them sometimes. Apparently, there are lots of them around here. Holly says they're from another century."

"Aliens? Gabriel talks about aliens."

"Sort of."

"They don't like me. They kicked me. Let's get out of here!"

I got up and barked. Trail likewise. Then we raced back down the hill to Holly's place. Holly let Trail in the house, but she shooed me away. I headed on back down Holly's meadow to the little ford that brought me to the safety of my own place and the vegetable gardens.

"Where've you been, Chucky?" Joanne asked.

I barked, and then lay close to her.

I lived part of the time in the new trailer now, but Rajah didn't like me being there. Often, I crossed the road and went back up the hill to the community cabin. Sometimes, I went to the timber frame of the house at the top of the far hill where the windmill stood. The house was rising rapidly, looking like a great pile of upright timbers. There were already two floors. I could tell that it was going to be bigger than Holly's place. I watched as the Amish people walked along the high beams, constantly banging in nails. I kept my distance from them, though, and barked if they came near. I just didn't trust those people.

It was still quite warm, but the woods all around the meadow turned a rich brown—almost orange. *The season's changing.* As the days went on, the leaves fell, baring the trees. Meanwhile, the house filled in with walls, and when the Amish people were not there, I sneaked inside and walked up and down the different levels. From the top level, beneath a big sky, I could see for miles down our valley that lay surrounded by those thickly wooded hills.

Peter came back with Bettine, the flute lady, one more time. When Joanne and Brian visited the house, I went with them. There was lots of siding inside the house now—according to Brian, pine on the high ceiling and some of the walls, and outside, cedar. "Only the Amish could have done this," Brian boasted. "You should've seen them up there. It's thirty-five feet high!"

"Do you think the house will be ready in December?" Bettine asked the foreman nervously.

Steve nodded.

One of the Amish men came into the great-room. I barked at him. Brian introduced the man to Bettine, "Danny Schwartz." I sniffed at his coarse, dark, woolen trousers. These Amish people didn't wear jeans like Brian and most of the community members—they wore trousers kept up by those suspenders.

Bettine reached into the bag she was carrying and took out her wooden flute. "Let me play for you?" she said. "You've done such a wonderful job," and then she repeated what she had said in a foreign language that I later learned to be German, and that the Amish seemed to understand. The sound of the flute drifted upward in the empty house— deep tones. *How beautiful!*

"What kind of flute is that?" Joanne asked.

"Native American," Bettine said.

"It's beautiful…ethereal."

"Yes, it sounds like two flutes at the same time."

I kept my eyes on Bettine while she was playing. *I want to live with this music.*

After a day or two, Bettine and Peter drove away, but this didn't stop me coming up the hill and watching the men work. Eventually, they added porches and wrap-around decks, lamps, and paint. *My house… soon, this will be my house…my kingdom!*

The sun was shining, and the ground was white with frost. I didn't notice the cold because of my thick coat. I heard the noise of a big truck drift down our valley and then up toward the house on the hill. I raced from the community cabin across to Holly's place to see what was happening. Trail joined me. At my house, I saw the red vehicle, with Peter and Bettine, along with the largest truck I'd ever seen. It had so many wheels. Strange men with black faces and wearing heavy anoraks, emerged. They looked around, shaking their heads. "Why d'ya ever leave St. Simons?" one of the men said. "It's freezin' here."

Peter and Bettine showed the black men into the house. When they came back out, the men started to unload things from the truck. Some boxes, they carried into the house, but many items of furniture they piled up on the deck. "I hope they finish the carpet in the great-room, tomorrow," Bettine said to Peter as she looked at the sofas and tables outside. Meanwhile, the great truck moved down behind the house, and the men started to unload items into the lower level. They completed the task by the mid-afternoon, but when they tried to drive from the lower level, the truck's wheels got stuck in the edge of the soft shale. The men cursed and shook their heads again. I heard one of them say, "Why here? Why Missouri…why Missouri?" *It sounds like he's saying, "Misery."*

Brian came up and tried to pull them out with the backhoe. The truck didn't budge. The sun turned red. Darkness fell before help came in the form of a vehicle with chains and winches, something like one I remembered seeing at Johnny's. Slowly, they succeeded in pulling the distressed truck out of the shale and back onto the drive. In no time, it pulled away with the two men. Brian drove the backhoe home by the light of its single working headlight. Bettine and Peter left in their red vehicle. Silence fell on the ghostly spectacle of the home with half its furnishings piled up on the outside decks. Even Trail said he must leave, but something drew me to this place. *My home. I must guard my home.*

I went up on the deck, lit now by a full moon and that myriad of stars—*those angels in the sky.* The air was crisp and clean. After peeing on the leg of a chair, I sat beside the furniture on the deck for a long time. *My kingdom.* Eventually, I wandered down the hill to the road and on to the trailer. Joanne filled my large bowl with a can of juicy meat that she made sure was nowhere near Rajah's bowl.

Early the next day, another clear and cold one, I independently went back to the house on the hill. It wasn't long before a blue van arrived with men that had been laying carpet. They busied themselves inside the house. I heard a lot of banging. Peter and Bettine came back in the red vehicle. I sat on the deck, and watched through the big, glass doors while the carpet was laid. By mid-afternoon it was completed. The carpet men, along with Brian and Leone, helped move the furniture into the house. As it grew dark, lights went on, and the candle bulbs from the chandeliers sparkled. Wall lanterns lit up, illuminating my deck. Bettine came out, and gave me a succulent piece of white chicken meat. I ran off with it and wolfed it down. When I returned to the deck, it was quite dark, but then that huge moon started to rise. I sat and surveyed my property. There were piles of shelf-rock on pallets littered in front of the house, upon all of which I had made my claim, but the rising moon now drew my attention. Its yellow orb splintered behind the ghostly branches of the oak trees, before climbing up into the dark sky…*our sky*. I didn't go back to the cabin that night. *No, I'm staying here. This is my task…this is* my *kingdom.*

Bettine and Peter came out on the deck to gaze at the moon and stars. I nuzzled up to them, tapping them with my right front paw. Peter smirked and said, "I think we may have acquired this dog."

"Go home, Chucky," Bettine said.

I looked up at her and stood my ground.

"Go home!" Peter repeated.

I rolled my eyes and looked away. *But this is* my *kingdom.* I didn't go far. I wasn't going to leave my new home.

Some two days later, Peter and Bettine drove away again, and didn't come back.

I must stay and guard the house. Although I went down to Joanne's trailer to get my food, I spent most my time at the house on the hill. *Are they ever coming back?* After about a week they did.

"Look, Chucky's still here," Peter said, when I greeted them at the front door, wagging my tail.

"You like it here, don't you?" Bettine suggested, rubbing me behind my ears. "We have chicken…perhaps we can find you some! Have you been here all the time we were in England?"

Where's that? I put my paw up, and looked into her eyes. *How can I tell you this is my kingdom?*

CHAPTER FOUR

How I got my Name

"Life is a joyride in all directions."

At the community cabin, Maryloulena and Leone kept fussing with the storage cabinets. It seemed they were becoming deeply concerned about this millenium thing they called "Y2K."

"We've only two days left," Maryloulena yelled at Joanne. "Why is it so important to you that we should have a housewarming party for Peter and Bettine up there that night? What'll you do when the millenium turns, and all the lights go out? Why is that house so important?"

"They'll bring a lot of new people to the community," Brian answered. Joanne just smiled. "They'll bring money and resources here," he continued. "That's what we need to create our independence."

"What we need is dedication to hard work and simple sustainability," Maryloulena quipped back.

They're talking about my people and my house. I need to get back there. I slipped out of the steaming cabin, and ran through our property until I was back at my house on the hill.

The following day, people drove up in the evening. I barked at their cars and watched through the big windows of the sliding doors as they came into the house. It looked so warm and inviting, with a log fire burning in the hearth at the base of the huge, shelf-rock chimney-piece. I wished I could be lying in front of that fire, but it was good at least to see in. The furniture was all arranged now—glittering gilt screens, sofas, chairs, tables, and all the things that I had so recently seen piled up on my deck in the moonlight. The carpet was almost the same color as me on a good day without mud. It was hard not to be covered in mud here, because all around the house there were only shale and mud.

I recognized my people from the community, but Taylor and his mother and father came. They didn't live here anymore, but they must have come back for this party. They arrived with the red-headed Sonja. Donnie and Kate drove up, the one's that always helped in the vegetable gardens. There were other people I didn't recognize. Joanne was busy introducing them to Peter and Bettine. They included a very large man, who sat down in a big chair and stayed there all evening. I think I heard his name… "Sartin." Oh, and there was Johnny! I gave out a little bark, but nobody heard me. I thought of Mama and the log cabin. *I would like to see Mama.* I sat down and crossed my paws. *Johnny's kitchen was so warm. It looks like it's warm in there, too, in front of that fire. I'd like to be inside with Johnny now.*

There was lots of merriment in the house, along with great platters of food. I sniffed at the big window. Later that night, I could see Brian and Sonja up on the loft balcony. They started to rain down glittering pieces of paper on all those below, who, by then, were wearing funny hats and blowing into noisy squeakers. The glittering pieces fell on the light carpet like colored snow. Maryloulena looked at her wrist, and sidled up to Leone. They raised their eyes to the big brass chandelier with all its candle-like lights that shone out as did the lamps on my deck. For a while, they all sang some strange song with words I didn't recognize. Joanne was smiling. Brian wasn't singing, however, but nervously stepped from foot to foot, looking up in solitude at the ceiling. Bettine joined Maryloulena and Leone. Then, after a few minutes, which I presume had taken us into this new millennium, as they kept calling it, Bettine went halfway up the stairs and started to play a golden flute. The people quieted down, and I could clearly hear the music. It drifted out onto my deck and down our valley. When she had finished playing, the sliding-glass door opened. Johnny came out into the cold night air with Joanne. "Chucky," she said. "You remember Johnny?"

My paws were up, and I stood in front of Johnny, scratching at his chest. I wanted to lick his face. I barked, proudly. *He's never really heard me bark. When I was a puppy, I did little more than squeak.* Now, I told him with a deep bark, "Take me to Mama," but I'm not sure he understood. He just rubbed my ears. I could smell Mama, and as I sniffed at his clothes, he caught on.

"You can smell Precious, can't you?"

"Yes!" I barked.

Peter came to the door. "Don't let him in," he said. "He'll wreck the carpet!" But, by now, I really knew I wasn't allowed inside. My task was to guard the house. Excitedly, I beat my paw against Johnny's chest.

"Well, no 'Y2K'," Johnny said to Joanne.

"No, it seems we'll live on," Joanne agreed. "But the preparation has set us up well as a sustainable community. We've lots of canned food and plenty of dried goods. We'll be able to live off 'Y2K' for a long time."

At length, Johnny stopped rubbing my ears.

"Down, Chucky!" Joanne said.

I sat on the deck again, and they went inside, but, oh, it felt good to have seen Johnny. He didn't come to the community meals as much now as he had when first I went to live with Joanne.

Two months later, the weather changed. The clear, cold nights gave way to rain. The area around the house on the hill became a quagmire. One night, while it rained, and I sat soaked on the deck, the bright flashes we often experienced later in the year, started to illuminate the sky. They were scary, especially when they got closer, accompanied by loud rumbling. Then the flashes became streaks, flying across the sky with forked tongues, and the rumblings became terrifying crashes. The angel-stars were hiding. *Perhaps the gods are fighting…fierce-barking like war.* I was about to abandon the house on the hill, for in the past, when these scary skies erupted, I'd been allowed inside the community cabin or down at Joanne's trailer. Momentarily, I took shelter under the red vehicle that Peter and Bettine always called, The Explorer. Then to my surprise, the front door of the house opened, letting out a streak of warm light into the night.

"Chucky!" Bettine called out loudly.

I poked my nose out from under the vehicle.

"There he is!" Peter exclaimed. "He's scared!"

I whimpered.

"Let's bring him in…but only in the mud room. He's really dirty now," Bettine said. "Fetch a towel."

Peter found a towel, and they both carried me in through the mud room door. Droplets of dirty water fell from my coat in pools onto the pristine terracotta tiles of the floor. They tried to towel me off, but they wouldn't let me into the warm kitchen. I spent that night in the mud room, but I did have food and water. The next morning, they let me out, and I barked around as I surveyed my kingdom. *My kingdom should include the inside of this house, not just that mud room.*

Little by little, I gained territory. First, it was the kitchen, where they put a barrier of chairs to stop me getting on the carpet area of the dining room, but I muscled my way through. I lay down on the soft carpet until they found me. Bettine just laughed. I knew then that it would not be long before I could gain access to the great-room. Once I did, I cast my eye on the big sofa. *Now, that would be comfortable.* It was! I was beginning to feel at home. They shooed me off the sofa, but they let me stay in the great-room with its hissing log fire. "I suppose now he's in, he really has become our dog," Peter said. "But I don't like that name, Chucky. Should we call him something else?"

A pink stuffed dog, wearing what Bettine said was a "Sherlock Holmes hat and a checked coat," was seated on the floor, along with some teddy bears. "Let's call him Orbit," Bettine said, while looking at the stuffed dog with its detective hat.

"After Orbit?"

"Yes. I don't travel much with my guitarist, Ricardo, anymore, so Orbit doesn't get to perform now, but he used to travel all over the country when we were on tour with *Young Audiences*. He and his companion had passports and everything. Children loved them when we performed in their schools. But, the stuffed dog was very spacey. That's why we called him Orbit. He was far out there."

"Orbit…" Peter repeated slowly. "You know that would be a good name, because Chucky still orbits around all over the community property. When we go there for an evening meal, guess who follows us all the way to the community cabin? Chucky." Peter flapped my ears. "Chucky, you're Orbit with the flying ears," he said, and from then on Bettine and Peter called me, Orbit.

Bettine was away a lot that winter. She always petted me before she left, but I got to know that when suitcases came out she was about to travel off to some place to play her flutes. Peter usually stayed behind, however, and we bonded.

Arlo started to build fences and dig holes for trees. And when warmer days came, Peter began to cut down all the tall, dry, winter grass. He used a noisy machine to do this that had flailing cords that spun very fast and cut down the brittle stems, grinding them up. I liked to follow him, and roll in the dry clippings. Our hill began to turn green instead of brown. Finally, he crossed to the other side of the road on the top of the ridge that led to our house. Back and forth, in fairly narrow swaths, he cut down the meadow grass, and occasionally rabbits ran from his path. I chased after them, but they were always too fast for me. Eventually, I gave up, and I sat down with my head resting on my crossed paws. It was a peaceful, sunny afternoon. I started to snooze.

I awoke to the sound of Peter yelling: "Arlo! Arlo!" Arlo's old car was rattling down the driveway. I saw what looked like wisps of smoke coming from the area where Peter stood screaming. Instinctively, I knew something was wrong, and bounded toward him. He started to pull his mowing machine backwards up the hill, and I could see orange flames darting out from underneath. Quickly, he abandoned the mower, and rushed back down the hill, frantically trying to stamp out the flickering flames that were taking hold in the dry grass. "Orbit!" Peter yelled, and I sensed fear in his voice. "Go back, Orbit!" Then, abandoning the spreading flames and thickening smoke, Peter ran up the hill and over to the house. I chased after him. He rushed into the house. I waited outside. I knew he was really scared. When he came out, he seemed to be shaking, but he came up to me and petted me. "Help is coming," he said.

The billowing gray and white smoke was now spreading farther and farther across the field, getting dangerously close to the woods below. In no time, the community people came. Then large, light-green trucks with flashing lights and sirens drove into the field. Men, wearing funny hats and slickers, got out and started dragging hoses. Maryloulena came over to us. "Are you okay?" she asked Peter.

"Somewhat shaken up."

They went into the house.

Trail came running toward me, and we barked together as we raced down to the scene of action. The flames were now climbing up the trees on the edge of the woods. Together, Trail and I barked at the flames. It was exciting, probably the most exciting thing that had happened since we started on our adventures together. The flames didn't respond to us, however, only becoming fiercer as they spread farther into the woods. By now, the men in the funny hats and slickers were busy dragging hoses down to the woods. Soon, they were spraying water. "This is fun!" I barked, and I ran up to one of them and stood up with my paws on his back as he focused the jet. My white coat was rapidly turning black like the burned undergrowth, and ash and smuts fell from the smoke billowing above us. The air smelled heavy, but I wasn't afraid…my heart was pounding with excitement. Closer to us, the others were beating at flames with shovels. Arlo seemed to be in charge, but like me he seemed to be enjoying it all. "Chucky!" he shouted. I could see he was laughing. *I'm Orbit.* I wanted to correct him.

After the sun set, the woods took on an orange hue. Trail and I barked as we joined in the line between Arlo and Leone. The inferno danced before us, but little by little, its area became reduced, controlled, and after about one hour, was left as just a few flickering flames among hollow logs.

"It should burn itself out now," Brian said knowingly.

"I'd watch it for a while," Clive suggested. "It depends on the wind."

The men with the fire trucks started to coil back their hoses. Holly and Bernadette brought out mugs of hot drinks for everyone, and it seemed we were all having somewhat of a party in the charred meadow. "Look at Trail and Orbit," Joanne said. "They're black." And, we seemed to get blacker as we played in that burned stubble. The ground crunched under our paws. Peter was thanking everyone, and blaming himself for what had happened. "But, the mower," he said, pointing back up the hill. "It's a miracle…it never exploded." He seemed a little less scared now.

At length, the trucks drove away, and everyone else left. Trail went home with Holly, but I, smelly and black, lay locked in the mud room.

About three hours later, Peter and I went out to check on the woods. "The fire's increasing again!" Peter shouted, and he rushed back to the house. Soon, the fire trucks were back. They didn't stay as long this time. "It'll burn itself out," one of the men said to Peter. "That's a hollow dead tree that's burning so fiercely, but it's safe."

He was right. Shortly after daylight, Peter and I were out there again. There was a lot of powdered ash on the ground, but the trees, somewhat blackened, still looked like trees, and only the dead ones seemed really charred. Wisps of smoke still rose from the site, but few flames licked at the charred forest floor.

"I hope the trees are alive," Peter said.

I looked up at the branches. *I expect so.*

Peter was trembling again, and I knew there was something wrong. *He's still afraid.* I realized that day, how important it was to be around him when he felt like this. *I must be his rock when he's afraid.* I nuzzled up to him, and he rubbed my ears. He looked up at the blackened meadow. "Well, at least we have it all mown now," he said. "The ashes will only enrich the grasses when they start to grow up this summer." I could tell from the tone of his voice and the smile that came across his face that I had somehow comforted him. "Now, how about you, Orbit? We're going to have to get you cleaned up," he said.

But it was days before I was white again. The oily ash stains just didn't fall off like dried mud. We were both right, however. Eventually, I became white, and the little green leaves broke out on the trees in those woods, hiding their blackened branches. The meadow grew rich, green grass and wild flowers, in which I loved to roll as the summer progressed. But, when Peter and I went on walks, we never ventured into those woods again.

For a while, Bettine came back from her travels, and excitedly, Joanne proposed that we should all go on a community outing. This became my first real adventure, riding in a vehicle. Brian and Joanne lifted me up into the back of the community van. At first, I was afraid, but when we were under way, I found the ride most soothing. I watched out of the window as the road receded behind us. Then I settled down and slept.

Sometime later, we pulled off the main roads onto a narrow dirt road.

"Wow! Billy and Loretta live in the boonies!" Leone chuckled.

"Nice," Maryloulena agreed.

I realized who they were, when we drove into a clearing where there was the strangest house. Taylor came up to the van when it stopped. I recognized his parents.

"Oh, you brought Chucky," Loretta noted.

"Don't let him in the house," Billy said when I jumped down from the van and Taylor patted my head.

Joanne hugged Loretta. "Bettine and Peter have changed his name to Orbit," she said.

Loretta rubbed my ears. "Sorry, Orbit," she repeated.

But when they all went into the house, I followed. After all, nobody had said Rajah couldn't go inside. Brian was carrying him.

The house smelled musty, and consisted of three connected round houses.

"Three geodesic domes with three different living areas," Billy explained.

Billy soon shooed me out, however, and it wasn't long before Brian came out and set Rajah down. I was still somewhat wary of Rajah.

I then observed some big birds running around outside. They were apparently called chickens. *I wonder if they are the same as the chicken we eat?* I decided to chase them. They didn't move nearly as fast as rabbits. I almost got one, except Brian intervened, slapping me on my snout.

"No! No Chucky!" he said severely.

I growled at him. *I guess I'm not supposed to chase chickens. Bummer!*

The smell of barbecue caught my attention instead, and I had hopes of chicken or steak as I lay among the wildflowers in the little clearing in front of this odd house. I was right, I got steak and chicken, and so did Rajah.

In the afternoon, we all went down to the river. This river was much more impressive than our Finley. The water fell over rocks and falls and swirled into a great cave in the bluff. It felt cool on this warm spring day, and the rushing water echoed in the cavern, as did the shrieks of

Maryloulena and Leone. Dick stayed on the far bank with Gabriel, but I followed the others into the cave, staying as close as I could to Peter and Bettine. We came out of the water onto a huge boulder in the middle of the cavern, and on the far side, lay a deep, dark pool. Way above, a little circle of light surrounded by green foliage sent a shaft down to where we were.

Brian dived into the pool. "Come on," he said. "Who's going to follow me to the top?" Bettine and Taylor dived in and joined Brian, and soon, Leone and Clive. I could tell, however, that Maryloulena didn't want to go, and just as in the woods, I could see that Peter was disturbed.

"I can't do those heights, and the water's too cold," he said to Maryloulena.

"Me neither," she agreed, and with me following, they waded back out of the cave into the warm sunlight and across the shallow river to join Dick and Gabriel on the other side.

I shook myself dry.

Not long after, we heard shrieks from way up at the top of the bluff. They'd made it...there they were...Brian, Taylor, Bettine, Clive, and Leone. They looked tiny among the fresh green leaves against the blue sky.

"Orbit!" Bettine shouted down to us.

I cocked my ears, panted loudly, and wagged my tail. I let out a little bark. *I hope they're all right?* Then I lay down on the riverbank, and listened to the buzz of insects, only to be disturbed momentarily, when Dick and Maryloulena took the naked Gabriel into the river. The little boy squealed with delight.

I dozed for a while to awake to the sound of others in the water. The rock climbers had returned. I rarely swam in the Finley, but this afternoon I ran into this river, and as it got deeper, flailed out to dog-paddle myself to Bettine. "Good doggie, Orbit," she said. "You're swimming! Isn't this beautiful here?" *I wonder if this is the place Mama talked about when first she told us of the river, the cave, the swirling water, the fresh green leaves of the riverbank foliage, and those high bluffs? Yes, it's beautiful.*

I was pretty much dry when Brian lifted me back into the van, but I wasn't afraid of the vehicle anymore, and I laid claim to my area. Rajah traveled up front. *Vans, cars, trucks, they can all take us to places. What a wonderful day this has been.*

"I think Chucky's settled down," Arlo said to Joanne as he looked back at me.

"It looks like it, but don't call him Chucky anymore. I think Peter and Bettine really want him to be Orbit now."

*Yes, I like Orbit...*And I fell asleep to the rhythm of the van.

CHAPTER FIVE

My Kingdom Grows

"Let others know when they have invaded your territory."

A LARGE YELLOW TRUCK DELIVERED gray lime. I sat and watched its contents fall out in a great heap. *Just for me. From on top of that pile I'll be able to look out over my kingdom.* As soon as the truck drove away, I went up to the pile, sniffed the musty powdery smell, and then peed on the lime, before ascending to the top of the pile, where I hollowed out my seat—my castle.

From my castle, I watched as Arlo, Leone, and Clive, started creating a great terrace from the pallets of shelf-rock. I then found out the purpose of the lime. Little by little, they wheel-barrowed it away from my pile. They used it to even the rough shale in which to set the flags of shelf-rock, but in one area of this growing terrace, they left a huge hole, in which grew monstrous weeds.

Meanwhile, Brian brought in several truckloads of earth. I followed him one day. He was taking it from near the area where the campsites were—where new community arrivals, Michael and Joy, and other occasional visitors, set up those tents close by the swimming hole. It was lush down there. This earth was darker. It had a pungent odor of…well, earth, more like that soil in the vegetable gardens. It smelled richer than the stony red clay that showed in gaping wounds all around our house. Back at our place, Brian dumped the contents, and the soil started to pile up on the western and southern side of the terrace. Peter kept picking stones from the area, and tried to remove the large quantity of roots and old timber that tumbled out from the dump truck with the earth. Trail often came up, and together we'd pull on the roots and sticks, thinking we were helping. Then we'd chase each other until one of us gave up, and dropped what we'd claimed. Sometimes, Trail tried to steal my seat atop the lime stack, and when he did, I barked fiercely until he climbed down, and I could regain my throne.

Looking down from my throne, I saw a tabby cat approach. At first, I just watched it, suspicious of the feline, but showing no hostility. The cat, however, started to lay claim to the deck in front of our great-room. When Bettine came out on the deck and fed it, that was just too much. As soon as she was back inside, I leapt down from my castle. The cat fled to the corner of the balcony deck. With a swipe of my tongue, I wolfed down the food Bettine had left on the saucer, then I lunged at the terrified cat, which jumped off the deck. I never saw it again.

Bettine was soon outside. "Orbit!" she shouted. "Bad dog! You can't chase the kitties. All animals are part of our world." I thought of the day I had chased Clive's cat. *He wasn't very pleased with me then. I suppose I'll just have to tolerate cats.* But, a great consoling thought came over me. *Here's the deal...if I tolerate these cats, I'll feel free to steal their food.*

A week or two later, a mostly white and gray, calico cat, ventured onto the balcony. I didn't attack her, and sooner or later, the cat was allowed in our house. I kept that deal most of our life together. She had to understand that I could eat her food. In fact, I got to like her cat food that Bettine or Peter set down on a dish in the kitchen not far from my big dog bowl. It seemed they wanted to name this cat, Alpha, so I called her Alpha, too. She was named after our house and land that everyone called, Alpha Meadows. She was never afraid of me, because I knew not to attack her. Actually, she was rather clever. She could walk on the cross-beams way up high in the great-room, like those Amish men, and in doing so she showed no fear. We became firm friends and shared many things throughout our lives, but we had this pact, I could always help myself to her food!

Joy and Michael brought another dog into our community. He had a black, curly coat that always seemed matted. He didn't mingle with me and Trail much, even staying his distance around the community cabin, although he seemed closer to Rajah than either of us. We learned his name was Bear. He seemed very devoted to Michael, and from time to time, he swam with him in the river. Trail and I weren't too keen on our river, but we liked the pond on top of the hill at Alpha Meadows. It was a great place to stand in and get cool. As the warm days of spring turned into summer, I liked the feel of the cool water on my stomach.

Peter brought home a big tiller and churned up the earth that Brian had delivered. Trail played a barking game with it, while Peter worked away. He'd follow at a safe distance and bark...bark...bark. I thought that a waste of energy, and retired to my castle atop of the lime pile. I didn't bark much. Barking seemed aggressive, and I only felt like being aggressive if I thought of the Amish. *There's just something about those Amish. They're not my kind of people. Trail thinks they take us animals too much for granted. They just want us to work for them. If they're not nice to animals I don't want to be nice to them. But, I guess that's my secret. Brian and Bettine seem to like those Amish.*

Eventually, the soil around the terrace was ready for planting. I'd watched Clive use a tilling machine on the vegetable gardens. When Peter tilled, he added black manure from green bags that smelled like cow pats, and bales of brown stuff that reminded me of the forest floor. He mixed them in with the earth before he started to plant, and his plants weren't like those in the vegetable garden. Some, were woody, and when they opened up, they had beautiful yellow, pink, and bronze-colored flowers.

"Those are beautiful," Bettine said. "What are they?"

"Deciduous azaleas," Peter replied.

Bettine sniffed at them, just like I would. "And these?" she said, pointing to a grouping of narrow, gray-leafed plants.

"Yarrow. It'll be yellow for about two months. They have it in England."

Peter often talks about England. Where is this England?

"I'm trying to plant this like an English garden," Peter continued, "a juxtaposition of spikes, mounds, and foliage." Plants with silver leaves looked velvety like a rabbit's ear, but Peter called them lamb's ear. In between, there were clumps of green. "These will be pink loosestrife," he said, "they're the same plant that we used to see growing around the lakes in Minnesota." He pointed to others. "They all look small at the moment, but they'll expand as the summer goes on."

Leone and Arlo came to work on the terrace. They were astounded to see the transformation, but it was only a tiny part of what was yet to come among those pallets of shelf-rock and the endless shale. As our garden grew, so did the grass. The meadow around the house was already half-way up my feet. A truck with a trailer drove up. A thin, tall man got out. He looked down to the terrace area and the flowerbed in front of it where Peter was working. Peter smiled when he saw him. This seemed to be something that made Peter happy. "My mower!" he shouted joyfully to Arlo and Leone. "Mr. Pennington's brought my mower!"

This mower seemed to be very important to Peter, so I thought I'd better investigate it. Mr. Pennington started to unload the red machine. I sniffed at him. *He's not Amish.* The man looked down at me. He seemed to have a kindly face. I looked up at him, *So what's so special about this mower?* When the mower was offloaded, Mr. Pennington started it up. It seemed very noisy, and I stepped back and barked.

"You'll love this," Mr. Pennington told Peter. "It's smooth….."
Smooth…my paw. It's scary!

He ran it out on the grass, away from the shale around the front of the house. The noise increased, and he started to cut the meadow. He ran the machine up and down, and I ventured into the cut area that smelled fresh…so clean, and I rolled around in the cuttings that left green sap on my white fur. Trail must have heard the noise. He came running up the hill and joined us. Peter then took his turn at the controls, and the mower wobbled all over the place. Peter didn't seem to be able to keep the machine running straight. "You'll get used to it," Mr. Pennington said. "You hardly have to move the ball at all." In a short while, Peter did get the hang of it. Mr. Pennington left, and Peter stayed on the mower for the rest of the day.

After that, I got used to Peter mowing, because he seemed to cut our grass areas every three or four days! At this time, he also seeded the oval area between the driveways in front of our house. Brian had spread soil there, and Peter added some of that forest-floor-like stuff—peat moss I think he called it. It wasn't long before the seeds opened and green grass started to show. As summer came on, I realized this was a nice, cool place to lie in the evenings, when the house cast a shadow on this new lawn. *This is* my *lawn.*

About this time, I started to play my game. If Peter or Bettine didn't bring me in from the oval lawn by sunset, I was off...yes, off in a flash. I knew this was the time that those community members were gathering for supper outside the cabin. As soon as Peter or Bettine tried to catch me, I ran away, as fast as I could, down past Holly's and Trail's place. My legs flew over the ground until I was up the hill the other side of the valley. Yes, the community members were just beginning to eat. Sometimes, Rajah and Bear, that black dog of Michael's, barked at me. I guess they didn't think I belonged there any more, but I knew Clive or Arlo would give me something from their plates. Rajah usually snarled. But one night, I could hardly believe my eyes when I saw Bear. He was nothing but skin, all his black hair shaved off. I felt so sorry for him—he looked dreadful.

"What's up with your hair?" I asked.

"It's my buzz cut."

I noticed Leone had no hair now, either.

"Buzz cut," Gabriel, the kid, said intuitively. He smiled, and looked up at his father. "My dad has a buzzzzz...."

I guess they all think it keeps them cool, but I hope nobody ever gives me a buzz cut.

Gabriel put his hand on my head and petted me. "Chucky should have a buzzzzz...." he said.

No, please no!

"Don't call him Chucky," Maryloulena said. "He's Orbit now."

Dick came over and rubbed my ears. *Yes, I like Dick.*

Eventually, after it had got quite dark, the light of headlights could be seen coming up the hill. It was Bettine's red Explorer. *They are coming to take me home.* Of course, I was happy to go...I had played the game. Before I jumped into the Explorer, I looked up at Bettine. "Don't give me a buzz," I pleaded, but I don't think she understood. Back we went to Alpha Meadows.

At night, I would sleep upstairs in the big loft bedroom with Peter and Bettine. I guarded the end of their bed, and often climbed onto the bed with them, but when the moon was full, I would scratch on the glass door leading out to a deck above the carport. I liked to sleep out there in the summer. I could hear all the frogs and crickets, and when the moon was full, it cast a silver sheen over the pond. Cool air rose up through the slats in the deck…that felt so good. In the moonlight, from up there, I could see even better than from the lime stack. That river of stars that looked almost like a cloud, wound across our sky. Bettine called it, the Milky Way, and it does look a bit like spilled milk. The stars aren't defined like they are to either side of this soft cloud. *Bettine's right. It looks a bit like spilled milk around Alpha's saucer after I've been lapping at it.*

Often in the evenings, Bettine played her flutes. I would lie with Peter in front of the warm fire and listen. The music those flutes made was so special to me. I knew it was sacred, somehow connecting us…Bettine and Peter, as humans, with me, as a dog…even me as a dog, connecting with the woods and the meadows of our place. Everything became one in that sacred sound. I felt, when I heard the flutes, as if I was somewhere different, like a land beyond the rainbow, where all color becomes so much brighter.

In fact, one afternoon, I tried to chase a rainbow after it rained, but I discovered they are elusive—they always move away from you. Trail and I both tried to reach the end of the rainbow, but we never could. Peter laughed when he saw us chasing the vibrant colors that arced through the sky to end up so close to us, but never in our reach. "If you ever catch it, you'll be rich, Orbit," he said as I lunged toward it. "Whoever can catch the end of a rainbow will find there a pot of gold." *Gold must be valuable, but not as valuable as the mystical beauty of the rainbow.*

That evening, after we'd been chasing the rainbow, I came in to the great-room.panting a lot after all the exertion. Bettine was very concerned. "Do you think Orbit's all right?" she said.

Peter lay down beside me. "I don't know…he seems very short of breath. Maybe there's something wrong with his heart. We can't take him to the vet until the morning."

They brought me a bowl of water, but I didn't pay much attention to it. I wasn't sure why they were so concerned. I felt quite normal. *My heart? This is just something that we dogs do. We breathe fast after exercise. How can I tell them I'm fine? I'm just annoyed that I can't find that pot of gold.*

"I'm going to call Johnny," Bettine said. "He'll know."

It wasn't long after that and there was a knock on the front door. By now, it was raining again, but there was Johnny in a wet coat. I jumped up, putting my paws on him. He ruffled my ears. His coat smelled like mildew, but his musk came through. *I'll never forget Johnny. Johnny always loved me when I was a pup.* I let out a faint bark.

"What's up?" Johnny asked, looking into my eyes.

"He seemed stressed, panting very fast," Bettine said.

"He and Trail had been running around barking at a rainbow," Peter added. "We're worried about his heart."

"Down, Orbit," Johnny said, putting his hands on me very gently. He listened to my chest. "Nothing wrong with Orbit," he said, "just hyper-ventilation…that's what they do. It's natural. He's fine."

Hyper-ventilation…yes, that's what they call it. That's just what we dogs do after we've been running around.

Johnny stood up. I put my paws up on his chest again, and stretched to my full height. "He's full-grown now," Johnny said. "I think he's bigger than Precious."

Lightning flashed and thunder rumbled. I never liked thunder. I jumped down from Johnny and coiled myself into my safe corner by the front door.

"Please forgive us for calling you out on this awful night," Peter said.

Bettine looked at Johnny. "We just love him so much and we didn't know what to do."

Then she turned to me. "It's all right, Orbit. Johnny says everything's all right." She started to play one of her flutes. There was another big clap of thunder, but I was less afraid, knowing they knew that I was all right.

Johnny left, but it had been good to see him.

I noticed something when the door closed that I hadn't seen before. There were various pictures in our house of other human beings, but on the wall to the left of the front door were two interesting portraits of a dog—a dog that looked very like me, but it wasn't me. I put my paws up on the wall and gazed at the portraits, tilting my head to one side and raising my ears. *I wonder who that dog is?* Looking back over my shoulder at Bettine, I let out a short bark.

"He recognizes my sketches of Woolly," Peter said. "Woolly had so many of the same traits as Orbit—and he had a similar coat…those same wondrous eyes…great wooly ears. He was an untrimmed standard poodle, but like Orbit, he had such human understanding."

Bettine smiled, "Look, he's still gazing at him."

I wish I'd known this dog. He has a kindred spirit. Maybe…? Could it be…? I feel one with his spirit, one with him. Perhaps he also knew Peter and Bettine? Could it be possible…that I…that he…that we, could all be one?

Peter laughed. "He definitely recognizes Woolly as another dog. My drawing can't be that bad. It was just a fifteen-minute sketch with a laundry marker, but it caught the essence of Woolly."

Essence. Yes…our essence.

There was a big flash of lightning, followed almost immediately by a very loud crack of thunder. I put down my paws, and nuzzled up to Bettine.

"That must be close," Peter said.

Heavy rain beat against the big glass windows of the great-room. When we went upstairs, I stayed with Bettine and Peter on the bed. This was no night to be outside on the deck.

A truckload of trees was delivered, their roots wrapped in balls. For a while, Arlo and Clive stopped working on the terrace, and set about planting these trees under Peter's guidance. I supervised from a distance, but when Arlo and Clive were gone, I investigated the trees. Most of them were planted in neat rows in the area between the windmill and our drive. The leaves on the tips of the few branches were a silvery green. I smelled them. *They are like the trees behind the community cabin on the way to Maryloulena and Leone's cabin. I think I heard Brian call those apples. Arlo seemed concerned because they never fruited. Maybe, these'll be better trees.*

In time, Arlo put little mesh circles around them. It made it harder for Trail and me to pee on them, but I heard Arlo say, "They are to keep the rabbits out." Yes, Trail and I used to chase rabbits up there from time to time, but less now that Peter keeps cutting the grass.

Clive dug trenches for pipes to take water to the new trees. He spent a lot of time playing with these pipes and testing them, and I noticed little feeders dripped water to each tree. Many other trees and shrubs started to be planted, and lines of these pipes were dug in all directions.

Lots of posts and rails arrived, and Arlo started to build a fence, enclosing the land with the pond in front of the house. Trail and I could climb through the fence, so it didn't stop us from getting to the pond, but it made me curious. *Why?* In the late summer, we found our answer. First, a white horse arrived with a thick mane. Bettine said, "He's a Foxtrotter," but she also said, "He reminds me of Icelandic horses I used to ride in Bavaria in my childhood." *So, we're going to have horses like Trail's place?*

At first, I was a little wary of this horse. Bettine named him Angelo. When she rode him on a beautiful September morning, the countryside dripping with dew, I followed at a distance. We went down to Trail's place, and my friend joined us. We continued to follow Bettine and Angelo up into the community woods, past the cabins, and into the oak forest. *It's beautiful up there this time of the year as the leaves begin to turn. Everything smells sweet, and sunlight falls in great shafts between the trees, catching the orange of old leaves and the rich red of shrubs growing along the edges of the trail. In the clearings, the grass is lush in the flush of fall growth after the long, hot summer, and clumps of tall, yellow flowers grow.* Trail and I found some deer bones and dragged them along with pride, but eventually it seemed just too much work, and we left them, and ran through the forest to catch up with Bettine and Angelo. Bettine looked over her shoulder and called out to us. My name echoed through the trees—"Orbit." *Oh, the freedom of it all. Life is great!* The arrival of this horse only made my kingdom grow. The sweet smell of fall had brought us a new blessing.

Later, one afternoon, a donkey was delivered—a stupid ass. He kicked at us with his hind legs, and his head and ears looked too big for his body. So, Trail and I barked at him, and chased him around the pond. Bettine named him Dominique. *A weird name.* Angelo seemed to team up with him, however, and when we went out on the trail, the wretched donkey made a dreadful noise that shattered the peace across the valley until we came back. *What a fool.*

Amish people arrived. With the Amish, more timber was delivered. Those noisy circular saws screeched again, and there were also sheets of metal. Concrete was poured. Hammers banged. A structure started to go up in Angelo's field. Those Amish men were always shouting at Dominique in that weird language they spoke, shooing him away. One day, I saw them throwing stones at him. *Yes, he is a fool.* But, I sensed that these men that smelled different were being unkind to him. *I don't like people who are unkind to us animals. We need to stick together.* I showed solidarity by barking almost continuously when the Amish were there. Of course, I could bark from the safety of my throne atop the lime pile, outside the new field and its feverish activity.

The new building turned out to be a house for Angelo and Dominique, and when it was finished it looked pretty. The doors had green patterns on them, and the roof sported a little turret with an iron piece carved like a chicken that turned in the wind. Peter and Bettine called them the stables, just like Holly and Bernadette. *That must be the name for horses' houses, but Angelo and Dominique don't seem to want to go in them much, except to poop!*

Fall turned to winter, and the next exciting development came when men in huge trucks delivered two sides of a house that they took down the hill and joined together. Suddenly, we had a log cabin—a little like Johnny's house. *Whose house is this going to be? Are Johnny and Mama going to come and live with us?*

Almost as soon as it was assembled, it snowed—really hard. The snow lasted for days. I found Brian talking to Bettine in the kitchen. "We can sled the furniture down," he said. "This is going to be fun."

And so a community project came about when several sleds, piled with sofas, tables, beds, and chairs, all held by ropes controlled by the community people, slowly slid down the hill to the log cabin. Meanwhile, we dogs cavorted in the snow. Rajah was almost buried. It was Bear that tried to bury him. There was fierce barking. But, on this occasion, Rajah was a good sport, and soon he was back wrestling with Bear. The snow smelled clean, and I loved to lick the ice out of my paws. Bear had his winter coat back now, and he looked so much better. I remembered how dreadful he'd looked in the summer. *No buzz cut for me. Peter and Bettine will never buzz cut me.*

The terrace was still not finished, as the fencing had taken priority. It would now have to wait until the spring. Part of that winter, both Peter and Bettine had to leave us. They said they were going on a journey to faraway places they named Tahiti, New Zealand, and Australia. Arlo was all excited that they were going to Australia, but the place names didn't mean much to me. So, that winter I spent some time with Rajah and his people in that steamy, busy cabin at the bottom of the hill.

CHAPTER SIX

Those Horses and Harry Trotter

"Sometimes I get into trouble, but it soon passes."

A NEW GIRL, SUSAN, CAME to live up in the community cabins in the spring. It seemed that young Job liked her looks, because he was always hanging around her. They came to dinner at Alpha Meadows with Joanne and Brian, and I overheard that Job and Susan were both now "First Responders" with the Fire Department—those men who had helped Peter when the field and woods were ablaze. At the table on our screen porch, Susan started to cry, telling us how the night before, when they'd gone out to someone's burning house, they'd seen the children outside watching their home disappear. "They were so helpless," she said. "All I could do was hug them." I liked her. She seemed my kind of person. *Yes, that's my task. I'm here to help humans, help them in every way that I can, but especially my people, Peter and Bettine.*

Bettine held out a large piece of boneless white chicken in front of my nose. I sniffed it, took it, then swallowed it whole. *Hmm…I like these dinners on the screen porch.* Ice cream followed, and I was allowed to clean off Bettine's plate. Satisfied, I licked my nose and paws. The big, red sun set behind the trees in the west, turning them a plum purple. The sounds of tree frogs and grasshoppers filled the air.

"This scene, at this time of night, always reminds me of the jungle in Brazil," Bettine said.

"How long were you in Brazil?" Joanne asked.

"Two years. I played in the symphony there; my little house was right on the edge of the jungle. I loved it. All sorts of animals used to visit me, and I'd play my flutes for them."

Yes, I could relate to that.

Red and purple streaks filled the darkening sky, and the night sounds of the insects grew louder. The angel-stars responded, opening their windows in the sky.

Brian smiled with his eyes. "There will be others up here," he said. "This place is the benchmark for what is to come."

In part through the help of Michael, that spring the terrace was finally finished, except for the hole in the shale where the weeds grew. My lime pile was reduced to nothing. A huge, folded sheet of heavy, black material was delivered on a truck. Arlo and Michael covered the bottom of the hole with old carpeting, and then molded this material into the hole, cementing the sides into the shelf-rock. They filled the space with water that spilled from hoses for a day-and-a-half, making a pond.

"It's a good thing we don't have to rely entirely on the windmill now," Peter said, his hands on his hips as he watched the hole filling. "That submersible electric pump in the well has its uses."

I wasn't sure what he was talking about, but when the pond was nearly full, I started to lap at the water. Bear went in.

"Get out of there!" Peter yelled.

Bear climbed out and looked at me, water dripping from his coat, but I thought it wiser not to do the same.

Later, a tank was set behind shelf-rock walls, and Clive worked pipes from the pond to the tank. Arlo set jagged stones from the top of the tank down to the pond. I came up to him while he was kneeling there, and sniffed at his work. He ruffled my head. "Chucky," he said in that twangy way he always spoke.

Why does he still call me Chucky. I'm Orbit! I walked away a little hurt, and seeing Alpha Cat the other side of the pond, I sidled up to her, nudged her, and then sat down with her to watch Arlo at work.

A magical moment came when water bubbled up from the pipes in the tank and spilled over the layers of rocks like rapids in a river, to empty into the pond, making a soothing sound.

Bettine and Peter came out on the terrace.

"What a beautiful waterfall," Bettine said. "Now we'll have to get fish."

"And water lilies," Peter added.

In time, both fish and water lilies came.

Meanwhile, Arlo created another waterfall in the corner cavity of the wall that he'd built to hide the concrete abutment running from the house and sheltering our terrace. Arlo and Peter threw buckets of water at the wall, and adjusted the rocks to see how the water fell.

"It's like tuning an instrument," Peter said.

He was right. I loved the sound of the water falling from the wall and splashing into a little pond—a pond, by the way, that was at perfect lapping height for me. The waterfall, or wall-fountain as Peter called it, *was* musical.

Great containers of climbing and trailing flowers stood at the base of the wooden posts that held up the decking around the house. On evenings when Peter and Bettine ate outside, and the moon rose over our terrace, Bettine often played her flutes. The waterfalls became her accompaniment. I lay on the terrace listening, and looking out at the growing flower gardens, contentedly knowing this was my kingdom.

It was about this time that a second horse arrived. An Amish boy unloaded him from a trailer, driven by someone who reminded me of Johnny—an Ozark man…big hands, tussled hair, rough skin, and wearing blue overalls. The boy said the horse's name was "Slim Jim." This horse became Peter's, and he joined Angelo and Dominique in the paddock with the stables. Now, Peter came riding with us.

One evening, after she played her flute for Peter and me, Bettine said, "You know I don't think we should call Slim Jim by that name. We should call him Amadeus."

Peter smiled. "After Mozart and the *Magic Flute?*"

"Wolfgang Amadeus Mozart," Bettine said, looking at me. "You see, Orbit, that was whose music I was just playing for you."

Play more! And as if she read my thinking, Bettine started to play again.

Arlo dug holes for posts and wire fencing on the far side of our driveway. I remembered that this was the area that had burned, but now it was all lush and green from Peter's incessant mowing. But, as I said before, I never saw Peter ever go down into the woods below that field again. I did, though. In fact, it was the scene of a crime I committed for which I still feel shame.

It all started when Michael came running up from Holly's place, chasing a little black pig. "Look! It's a pig, a real live pig!" he said excitedly. I intercepted the pig. The animal let me sniff him, even smiled at me with laughing little eyes. I was much bigger than he was, but he wasn't afraid. Peter and Bettine joined us. "He must be somebody's pet," Michael said. "Look, he's not even afraid of Orbit."

"A pet?" Peter questioned.

"Potbelly pigs like this make great pets," Michael assured him. "What should we do with him?"

"If he belongs to someone, they'll come looking for him."

"Let's keep him on the deck for now," Bettine suggested. And so it was that a black potbelly pig came to live on our deck. Bettine fed him scraps, and she gave him a blanket. "We'll call him Harry Trotter," she said.

Michael laughed.

During the next few days, the pig got a lot of attention. The community people all came to see him…even Gabriel.

"He's named after Harry Potter," Maryloulena explained to the child.

"Is he a wizard?" Gabriel asked

"Maybe," Maryloulena said with knowing eyes.

Who's this Harry Potter? I nuzzled up between Maryloulena and Gabriel, as if seeking an answer, but the little boy just looked at me and said, "You're not a wizard, Chucky."

"Orbit," Maryloulena corrected him.

That's better.

"Orbit's got big," the boy said.

Joanne chuckled. "Harry Trotter will get big, too. Potbelly pigs grow really fast."

It got a little smelly on the deck after a day or two, and Harry Trotter was released, but he never went far. It seemed he knew he'd found a new family. He befriended Angelo and Dominique, but Amadeus seemed wary of him. And so, through the summer, Harry hung out with us.

I remained curious about the creature, but at first, Trail didn't pay a lot of attention to him. Then came the day of the crime. It was one of those really hot, late-summer days. Trail came to visit, and we persuaded Harry to join us on an adventure down into the coolness of the woods, adjacent to the fields where Holly kept her horses. Harry never normally went that far, staying pretty much up around the stables and the lawn below Peter's terrace gardens. At first, Harry held back, but we coaxed him to cross the meadow the far side of our hill. The smell of the woods, with their floor of decaying leaves, beckoned. Trail made fun of Harry, as the pig, now quite a bit bigger than when he had first arrived, struggled through the underbrush, snorting at the branches and trunks of fallen trees. Trail ran behind him, barking. Harry squealed and jumped. The pig started to run down the hill, but I was already ahead of him. I turned to stop him. I remembered what Mama had said—"We're Great Pyrenees, we used to herd sheep in Spain." The creature squealed again, and circled in the area between us. This was fun. Then something suddenly came over me. I pounced on the pig. I smelled something familiar, something delicious—his ears. They were quite large, and reminded me of some treats that Bettine had once given me. Trail pounced on the pig, too. I had my teeth into one of his ears. It ripped. Harry let out a terrible scream. Trail barked fiercely, and took a bite at his other ear. His bite was much smaller than mine—just a little circular nick on the end—but the ear I'd bitten was now bleeding profusely. I let go. I looked at Trail, who also let go. Harry fled.

I saw there was blood on my paw and chest. *This isn't good.* Immediately, there arose a feeling of deep shame and remorse in my stomach. We could still hear little whimpering squeals from the woods below us. "We've hurt our friend," I said to Trail. "He's not a dead deer or a smelly armadillo. He's not one of those pesky rabbits. He's one of us…part of *our* family."

"How can we make amends?" Trail said deeply, with his vibrant tail now hanging limp between his legs.

"I don't know, I feel dreadful," I said.

"Me, too," Trail agreed.

Slowly, we made our way through the underbrush below the oak trees and back up to the meadow on top of the hill. Trail then went his way, and I went mine. It was dusk when I finally saw Harry Trotter again. He eventually made his way back up the hill and was in the paddock with Angelo, who was licking the little pig's wounds…at least, until that frisky donkey chased him away.

How am I going to explain this to Peter and Bettine? I couldn't hide the blood on my nose and chest, although I licked at my paws.

"Where've you been? What was all that squealing?" Peter asked. "You were with Harry Trotter by the stables. Where's Harry Trotter?"

I gave an apologetic woof.

"There's Harry!" Bettine shouted. "He's in the field with Angelo."

Peter and Bettine went through the gate, but I hung back.

When they returned, I knew I was in trouble.

"Bad dog!" Bettine said. "You bit his ear! That's why you have all this blood on your nose and chest."

I lowered my eyes.

"Well, it might have been Trail," Peter said.

I gave Peter a sideways glance.

"Mud room!" Bettine said.

I knew what that meant…*Confinement.*

During the next few days, a fence was constructed marking off a corner of the horses' field. This became Harry Trotter's pen. The horses were very curious, as they really seemed to like Harry. When he was placed in the pen, they came up to their side and put their heads over the fence, while Harry stood up with his feet on the wire. They rubbed noses, while the pig's curly, little tail wagged. I felt jealous, because I was quite contrite. I knew it was my task now to protect the pig, too, as part of our family. Harry was still wary of me, however, even though I often went up to the pen to try to make amends. But, little by little, he came to accept me again.

My biggest loss was Trail. He simply disappeared. He never came up to visit me. I wondered why. At length, I made my way down the hill to Holly's place. A picket fence had been built in front of the house, behind which Trail was penned. Holly came out. "Go home!" she shouted. I seemed no longer to be welcome. From then on, Trail and I saw each other only at barbecue picnics and cookouts in the community. No longer could we roam freely together wherever we chose. *Was it Trail's idea or was it mine to tempt the pig down into the woods? I really don't know. I guess we both just instinctively decided to corner poor Harry. I've learned a lesson. I'll try, oh I'll try to make amends!*

I don't really know what happened to me next, but I know it was traumatic. Joanne had come up to see Harry Trotter, concerned about his ears. We went to his pen. I sat on the grass, while they checked on the pig.

Joanne looked at me. "You know, we never did have Orbit neutered," she said. "He really should be done before he gets too old. It will quiet him down. Then this kind of thing won't happen."

Neutered. What's that?

"It would save us a lot of potential trouble in the neighborhood, too," Joanne continued. "Some of these people out here would think nothing of shooting him if he strays on their land and becomes aggressive."

Bettine looked at me with an expression that mixed fear and sympathy...a smile suppressed behind a tight lip. "Will it hurt him?" she asked.

"They'll put him under," Joanne said in a matter-of-fact sort of way. "We don't want some sort of a law-suit against the community should he upset our neighbors. It really has to be done."

"But then, he could never be a father?" Bettine pleaded.

"Well, do you want to breed him?"

"Well, you never know, it might just happen."

"Exactly! That's why we have to protect ourselves, at least as long as he is free to orbit around the area."

Bettine looked at Peter.

"I suppose we'd better take him to the vet," Peter agreed.

Bettine looked at me again, and quietly said, "Orbit."

I knew this was serious stuff. The next day, they took me to a place in Diggins, just off the highway between Seymour and Fordland.

When I got there, I could smell Dr. Espey, the man who came out once in a while to check on our horses. There were also odors of all

sorts of other dogs mixed in with a smell of urine and sweet-smelling…
something…I really didn't know what, I had never encountered this
sickly-sweet smell before.

They took me into a room and weighed me. Dr. Espey prodded me
and told me I was a "good dog." We waited there until he came back and
pricked me with a needle. I almost immediately felt sleepy…actually it
was a good feeling, and then…everything seemed to go blank.

When I woke up, bandages swathed my backside, and when I tried to
walk, it felt sore. *What's this? Some sort of punishment for my crime?* But
I soon dismissed this thought when I saw Bettine and Peter, who looked
at me very lovingly, and gently patted my head. "Orbit, we can go home
now," Bettine said.

They carried me into the Explorer. Soon, we were back in my familiar
kingdom. I had to put up with the bandages for about two days, but the
soreness quickly went away. During this time, I wasn't allowed in the
house. When Maryloulena, Leone, and Gabriel, came to our terrace for
dinner, the child stared at me, grinned, and then said excitedly, "Look,
Orbit's wearing a diaper!" I could sense he was laughing at me, or maybe
with me. The half-naked kid was usually wearing some sort of similar
bandage around his backside! After I'd tried many times to tear and lick
the bandages away, Bettine and Peter took the smelly item off. I felt free
again…*Oh, what a relief!*

It was apparently Holly's suggestion, but it didn't work for me. Peter and
Bettine led me into the orchard with its big deer fence around it, and
then shut the gate on me. *They're locking me up in here, just like they've
locked up Trail.* When they drove off in the Explorer, I walked all around
the perimeter of the fence. I saw a spot where some critters had pushed
up the netting. I sniffed at it. *Not Armadillo…Rabbits!* I then started to
push at the netting with my snout. The hole got bigger. Soon, I could get
my head through, and I pushed up from my neck and shoulders until
the netting easily started to buckle. It wasn't long before I could slither
through. I was free. *They'll never cage me!*

I must admit that when Peter and Bettine came back in the Explorer and saw me on the oval lawn, they just laughed. "Orbit will always be free," Bettine said after she got out: "I promise you, Orby, you'll always be free."

Without Trail, I started to explore the woods to our north. It was about this time that work started on another house. After foundations were laid, the Amish came back. Brian was terribly excited about this house. It was being built, so he said, like an Amish barn. "There are no nails," he explained to Peter and Bettine. "All the frames are pegged together in the old-fashioned way."

We all became very curious about this structure, and we were there for the raising of the first frame. The Amish men pulled it up using ropes, and as in the building of our house, Danny Schwartz was in charge. One by one, some five gigantic frames were raised. Rajah and I watched in awe, but we kept our distance from the Amish, and from time to time, we wandered off into the woods or chased rabbits. When I ran after a rabbit, Peter shouted, "There go the Orbit ears." *I guess my ears flap when I run.*

One time, Rajah ran off and he didn't come back. Brian was very concerned. "Maybe he met a cayote," he said. Animals in the woods sometimes howled at night. *Perhaps they're cayotes?*

A few days later, however, Brian came to the building site. Rajah was with him.

"You've found him!" Arlo said.

"He was in Seymour. Wes found him."

"At the post office?"

"Yes. He had him in the back. Somebody had handed him in, and Wes knew the dog was Rajah." Brian grinned. "You see, Arlo, that's one good reason for living in small-town America. Everyone knows you and your dog, especially the postmaster."

Arlo smiled. "Same in Australia, mate."

Rajah ran up to me and wagged his tail, pleased to see me. I sniffed him. *I'm glad he's back, even if we are not the best of friends. He's part of our family, too.*

Brian and Arlo went to work on the beams. This interesting house was being built for a friendly man named Fred Johanssen. He came to visit a few times, even stayed with us once at Alpha Meadows, but he left most the work in the hands of Brian and Danny Schwartz. Apparently, he first met Peter and Bettine on some course in Colorado, at the time

they were living in Minnesota. *I have no idea where these places are.*
They often laughed about the odd little hotel where the course had been
held. Later, Fred met Kiri on one of those courses in Florida that our
community members seemed to always attend in the winter. They said
she was "Korean," whatever that means. *To me people are people.* Brian
convinced them to buy land and join our community. Kiri came to stay
while they were building the new house.

After the frames were up, Clive, Brian, and Arlo, took over most of
the remaining building work. It was a curious house with a huge hall
and wide staircase that led to what was more like a small apartment. A
narrower staircase led down to a series of guest bedrooms. Fred said he
designed it so that spiritual courses could be held there. Already, many
courses were held at our house.

I enjoyed the courses. I saw how they made the people glow, and
in turn that made me feel good. Often, toward the end of the courses,
when everyone seemed so free and happy, the people came out onto our
oval lawn, taking off their shoes and making a circle. Then they danced
to haunting music. I liked to join them, breaking into the middle of the
circle. Often, I pawed Peter or Bettine, and sometimes Dick, while they
swayed to the melodies. Nobody spoke, the only sounds were the haunting
music and the rustle of skirts. Joanne called these, Sacred Dances. I wasn't
sure I wanted the courses to move to Fred's house.

When furniture arrived for his new house, it was decidedly different…
apparently Korean like Kiri. The front door was open all day as men
unloaded the pieces from a big truck. I snuck inside and watched the
big, empty room with its high beams begin to fill. I looked up. *Beams…
inspired by* our *house.*

Kiri was definitely in charge. Eventually, she chased me out. "Go,
Orbit! Go! You're in the way!"

Fred and Kiri named their house Laughing Dragons Lodge after three
carved creatures with wings and laughing faces that sat on a huge table
in that great-room, but I was never sure if it was a part of my kingdom.
Sometimes, I looked in through the windows from the decks that wrapped
around three sides of the building, but if Kiri saw me, she shooed me away.
Kiri was often not there, however, and if Fred saw me outside, *he* would

invite me in. Often he shared his food with me, and we would sit on his sofa together and watch moving pictures on this big screen.

Yet another house started to be built at this time. It was just over the hill from our place, not far from the woods of my crime. Steve Owens was supervising again, but there were less Amish around on this project. Like all our houses, it was built into the side of the hill. Two young women came to live there. They both had the same name…Michelle, so everyone called them, M and M. They seemed to be friends of Holly's. They kept to themselves and didn't attend our courses, but they were friendly enough if I ventured down to visit them. I met their dogs, and sometimes these women invited me in to watch moving pictures on their big screen, too. They always seemed to be watching the same thing, something they called *Pirates of the Caribbean.* I knew something about these pirates, because Gabriel talked about them at the community cabin. He thought he was some little boy called Peter Pan, and he talked about a pirate named Captain Hook. *Gabriel…he's a funny little creature. He never seems to grow up, but apparently Peter Pan doesn't either.*

CHAPTER SEVEN

Concerts, Courses, and Social Gatherings

"Oh, I am so happy, and my wagging tail shakes my whole body."

BY THE EARLY FALL OF that first summer, our flower beds already began to look good. A young woman came to stay with us whose name was Lori. She had a large wooden instrument that I learned was called a Celtic harp. I warmed to her when she played the harp in our great-room at the same time that Bettine played her flutes. The mingling of the sounds was beautiful, enough to make me want to sing along with them. I tried it out. Bettine put down her flute. "Orbit, you're singing!" she exclaimed. Lori laughed. "Lori, Orbit *is* singing!" Bettine repeated. "He really is." *Yes, I'm following the music. I can't help it. It's so beautiful.*

Bettine then started to play on one of her smallest flutes that made the highest notes. I picked up the tune and repeated the phrasing with her. "Good dog, Orbit! You're really singing with us!" Bettine repeated.

Meanwhile, Peter was busy setting out many green chairs in the garden. It was a hot September day.

"Orbit could sing with us at the concert," Bettine said.

Lori shook her head with a grimace. "You don't know that he'll do that again."

"We could try."

"I don't think so. That's too spacey."

I just sat, looking at them with doleful eyes. Bettine opened the door onto the deck.

"Do you think they'll hear us all right?" Lori questioned, when she saw the chairs lined up between the flowerbeds, beyond the terrace, and even out to the grass of the sloping lawn.

"Let's see," Bettine said, and she started to play her flute.

Peter looked up.

"Can you hear all right?" Bettine shouted down.

The air was very still in the heat of mid-afternoon. "It sounds beautiful," Peter answered. "I'll walk back farther. Keep playing." Lori started to play her harp at the same time. "You know what," Peter shouted back, "the huge glass windows of the great-room are acting as a sounding board. They're projecting the music out over the whole garden."

I left the deck and wandered down to the terrace. The notes of the beautiful music drifted overhead. *Something's going to be happening here. A concert? Something to do with this beautiful music.* I remembered how earlier in the summer a man had come to stay. He liked me a lot. He was always rubbing my ears. His name was Brian Beaton. I remember Brian saying to Peter and Bettine, "Your property would be a wonderful place to have garden concerts. You should have a concert series." *Perhaps now, we're going to start a series of garden concerts?* I was excited at the prospect, and even more so when Peter started to make all sorts of sandwiches, and set up tables on the terrace with glasses, bottles, and jugs of cool-looking drinks. *We're going to have a concert and a party.*

It was still pretty warm when people started to come, but they kept coming…not just the community members, but people whom I'd never seen before. As I saw them looking around the house and gardens, I could see that many of them were curious. *They want to know about my kingdom. Well, I'll show them around.* I went down to the terrace and ingratiated myself to them. I recognized Mr. Pennington and several other people whom I'd seen in Seymour when I went into town with Peter and Bettine, including Wes, the kind man at the post office. Then, Johnny came. My throat squeaked. *Johnny! Mama!* I gave out a little bark. The people congregating on the terrace, were eating the sandwiches, and filling up their glasses, when after a while, Peter came out on the balcony. He was dressed in a beautiful silk shirt. "If you would like to take your seats," he announced in a clear, loud voice, "the performance will begin in five minutes."

Johnny fed me a sandwich, and I carried it off and sat down by the wall-fountain. *This is going to be some party.* The people started to seat themselves in the garden, facing the balcony deck and great façade of the house. *A concert...a concert in my kingdom!*

Peter came out again through the sliding-glass doors. He thanked everyone for coming, and then introduced Lori. Once Lori was seated at her harp, he continued, "And now, ladies and gentlemen, in this beautiful setting, let's enjoy the wonderful music of Lori Robinson and Bettine Clemen."

Bettine nodded to Lori from the doorway, and the music began—such magical music. As I looked around, I could see that the people were enraptured, just like me. Where I was sitting, close to the wall-fountain, I could also hear the music of the water. In an extraordinary way, from the beauty of our terrace, the flute, harp, and waterfalls, meshed. *Now, I understand why this garden is so important to Peter.* At the end of the concert, the sun was already setting and the moon rising...a scenario that would be repeated many times on our terrace as countless people experienced the beauty.

A year later, when the garden was in full bloom, Lori came back for another concert. This time, however, there was a third performer, a jolly, rotund man, who played gongs—great circular discs that he hit with sticks and brushes. They made interesting vibrating sounds that rang through my ears. Along with them, Bettine played haunting music on wooden flutes and multiple pipes that sounded very mysterious. She called it, Native American music, but I wasn't sure what that meant. It was very different. Lori sang as she played her harp—lilting sounds. And... the waterfalls played. The people were as enraptured as the year before.

As the gardens matured, other gatherings took place. Frequently, people for the courses came to our house and garden. Many stayed in our log-cabin guesthouse or at Fred's house. Others camped down by the river. At times, these courses were very quiet, the people wandering around the garden, examining leaves and blooms, or just staring at the waterfall or watching the fish.

The community also made a big event out of July 4—apparently some sort of national holiday, although Peter said, "It's my birthday." We all went down to the area where Michael, Clive, and Arlo had been constructing that pavilion, now flanging out from the old silo tower. The building never was completed, but we did have some large gatherings there. On these occasions, all of us community dogs were reunited, and we would run off together, and sniff in the tents down by the river. Bear always swam, but then this area was *his* kingdom. After the picnic, all of a sudden there was a whirring sound similar to a lawn mower, coming from the far side of the trees, but from above. Bear and I turned and looked up. This contraption, like a big bird, flew over us, and a man perched on a little seat waved at us.

"It's Jack!" Brian shouted.

"Come and join us!" Joanne yelled through cupped hands.

The flying machine circled around as we all followed its path. Round it came again, and then lower, until it landed in our field.

Jack got out.

"You're in time for the fireworks," Brian said.

As it started to get dark, Job and Brian lit fuses and presented a frightening display of noisy and terrifying explosions that made awesome patterns in the sky. We dogs hated these explosions. I could hear Trail whimpering, and even Rajah was cowed. I was scared, too. It was worse than thunder. I slunk over to the Explorer, and Peter let me in, where I cowed on the back seat. Trail got so scared that Holly had to take him home. Bear was probably the least of us to be affected. He just sat beside Michael and Joy, and watched those patterns in the sky.

The following spring, not long after everyone had come back from one of those Florida courses, Al and Julie came to live with us. Actually, they lived in our guesthouse. They had a dog named Timo. He was a wise dog, but he was totally devoted to this Al and Julie. It was hard to get to know Timo very well, because he kept himself pretty much down at the guesthouse, but Al and Julie often came up to our house during those summer months. Like Joanne and Bettine, they taught at the courses.

It was during that spring, too, that our community land nearly doubled. Joanne's father bought the neighboring farm, and he and his wife spent a good part of the summer there. They called it, Finley Farms. Joanne's mother came to the courses, but her father didn't, however, they both often came to dinner at Alpha Meadows. They loved our place, and they always petted me. They often talked about what they might do with their new land. I thought they were both really great people. They loved Bettine's music. Sometimes, Bettine and Peter would take the horses riding at Finley Farms. Of course, I'd go with them.

The land at Finley Farms was much more open than up behind the community cabins, and we had to go through the Little Finley river. Angelo loved to splash everyone when we crossed the ford, and I got very wet, too. Amadeus, however, was a little more wary of the running water. Sometimes, I barked behind him to get him to move. The other side of the river, we could run up through a big field with views down our valley and back to Alpha Meadows. You could see our windmill, and the sun reflecting off the big windows of our great-room. I realized that where we now were was what we could see when we looked out of the great-room over the woods to sun-splashed hills leading up to the distant ridge. This was heaven…I felt so free, and the rides made Bettine and Peter so happy, too. In fact, on one beautiful summer morning when we were out at Finley Farms, Peter and Bettine stopped by a little water-meadow and held hands. I stood close by, watching them. This seemed to be a sacred moment. "Today, on this our anniversary, June nineteenth, I ask you once again to marry me," Peter said solemnly, although his eyes were smiling with happiness.

Bettine was looking into them. "Of course, and will you continue to be my beloved husband?"

"Yes."

I could sense them squeezing their clasped hands. Angelo started to paw at the ground.

"You're a witness, Angelo," Bettine said, letting go of Peter's hand and pulling on the rein, "Now, lift up your head!"

I gave a little bark.

"You, too, Orbit, you've just witnessed something very beautiful."

I knew it, because I could see happy tears running from the corners of their eyes that they tried to wipe away with the backs of their hands.

"All right, Angelo," Bettine said, "let's go up the hill."

I followed them, my ears flying, as Angelo and Amadeus galloped off to the higher ground. *So free...so free!.*

There were many more people at the July fourth picnic that summer, and a lot stayed on in tents and campers for a couple of months until there was this huge gathering at the pavilion in the fall.

The trees were beginning to turn yellow and orange when the day came. The pavilion looked better than I'd ever seen it—there were lots of flowers spilling out of barrels and growing up trellises around the pillars, somewhat like we had at Alpha Meadows, but I suppose that wasn't surprising, because apparently Peter planted them for this special event. In fact, there were flowerbeds in several areas around the pavilion that I never saw planted before, and we dogs laid our claim to them much to Joy's annoyance, as she was the main person working in those flowerbeds. Actually, she used to help Peter in our garden, too. For this event, the grass field where the pavilion stood was all beautifully mown just like our grass, and it felt good when we rolled on our backs. After all the people were seated in front of the pavilion, Brian made a long speech from the stage, and Peter, too. Peter said something about two hills, and pointed up toward our place and then to the hill above Finley Farms. I'm not sure what he was talking about. We dogs just wandered among the people during these speeches, but I heard the words "Sage Hill Institute" mentioned a lot. After this, the people all sat in little groups and discussed things intensely. I heard Bettine say, "This meeting is a seminar about our future as a community." This event seemed to be important. *Sage Hill Institute...a teaching center, here at our community? I hope that won't mean buildings up on those hills? That's where we go with the horses.*

Some of the people who came were staying at our guesthouse with Al and Julie, others were at Laughing Dragons' Lodge, and many were up in the community cabins, with a lot more sleeping in those tents and campers. I think it was the biggest gathering we ever had. People came from all over the country, and some, even from other far away places around the world. Many of them talked about the big concert Bettine had given the night before, and they recognized me, because, apparently, I had sung during the concert from a large overhead screen on a vast stage at a place called Hammons Hall in Springfield. They also talked about a man named Neale, who'd spoken there after the concert with a neat lady named Thea, all part of this special event. Thea was living with her husband in a huge camper parked just the other side of Angelo's and Amadeus' field. I liked her. She let me visit with them in the camper, and she gave me treats. But, it was a strange time. Just a few days before, something terrible had happened that everyone called "Nine-Eleven."

I was out with Peter and Bettine, who were riding that September morning. We came to Joanne's house, a farmhouse she was converting on another neighboring farm she had apparently bought from Sartin, increasing yet more the size of our community land. She told us about this terrible accident in a place called New York. When we got home, Peter and Bettine quickly unsaddled the horses, and we rushed inside. They turned on that small screen in the great-room. Our screen was much smaller than that of Fred's or M and M's. They stayed watching the screen much of the day, while I slept.

At the pavilion meeting, Leone mentioned this "Nine-Eleven" several times. *I wonder what happened? Something about airplanes flying into buildings that collapsed and killed many, many people. That's sad.*

There were other less serious occasions, when people just came to visit us at our house. Every summer, for two days, our place was thrown open to lots of people I had never seen before. They just came to see our gardens. Alpha Meadows was apparently on some sort of a tour program associated with ponds. Well, we did have a big pond and that beautiful wall-fountain. Many pink water lilies now bloomed in the pond, and even the pond in the horses' field was covered in white water lilies. There were now so many flowers in our garden, and a constant buzzing of bees. Sometimes, little birds with long beaks and fast-moving wings hovered around our big tubs planted out on the deck—Joanne and Brian called them humming birds. We also had a lot of butterflies. There were big bushes that Peter called butterfly bushes that seemed to attract them. They had long flowers in pink, purple, and white. He said, "They grow well here because they like stony soil." Our land is stony. I felt proud. *This is* my *garden.* I wandered to the wall-fountain and took a drink from the small pond. These visitors loved our place. Bettine nearly always played some of her flutes for them, while Peter fed the visitors light refreshments.

Other garden groups visited, and on one weekend, a very funny man and his two children from Branson came to stay in our guesthouse. Apparently, he was a famous Russian comedian whom Peter had known for many years. They called him, Yakov Smirnoff. He and I just bonded right away. He said I glowed. He even said, "Orbit's not just a dog; he's a spiritual being." *I wonder what that means?*

The garden always seemed to make Peter happy. *It's my task to keep Bettine and Peter happy, too, but so often Bettine has to go away on concert tours. I know Peter gets lonely. We both miss her when she has to travel.*

All of a sudden the music of the flute started. Bettine nodded her head and walked toward me. She was playing one of my favorite tunes, which she said came from *Carmen.* I started to sing along with her. I could see the amazement on Yakov Smirnoff's face.

There was one time, however, when a garden group was coming, and Peter had put out sandwiches and cookies for them, that I found the plates on a table under the screen porch and helped myself, not knowing there was going to be a party! I could feel that no-one was very pleased.

One of the things I enjoyed most on summer evenings in our garden, was when Peter and Bettine invited people to dinner on our terrace. Of course, often they were visitors to the community, but there were others…ladies in red hats, people who liked to dress up, horse people, smaller garden groups, and just obvious friends of Peter and Bettine. Peter set the tables with large white cloths that had shimmering patterns. He placed oil lamps and ornaments on them, and then great bowls of fruit, lots of china and glass, including stemmed glasses that he called, crystal, that sparkled in the sunlight. The wrought-iron chairs all had matching cushions, and there were linens that matched them, too. Beautiful flowers trailed among the table ornaments and picked up the colors of the gardens all around.

Sometimes, a pretty lady came to the house to help prepare dishes for our guests—salads, exotic entrees, and ice cream and fruit desserts. Her name was Laura…Laura Lucey. I'd sit beside the table on the terrace, and I usually lucked out. Other times, Peter and Bettine cooked steak or chicken on the grill. That made my nose twitch, but Bettine always made sure I got my fair share, actually a lot more than she gave herself. Sometimes, in the moonlight I would see a deer, or I would hear that strange munching noise of an armadillo. Off I'd go with flying ears, barking for all I was worth. *Well, these guests had to know that I really am a dog.*

One evening, when our guests left, Peter and Bettine danced on the terrace to the sultry sounds of a lady, who apparently sang in French, a language unknown to me. "Francoise Hardy," Bettine said. Peter and Bettine looked so happy. I nuzzled up to them, and put my paws up so we could all dance together, just like I did when they had that dancing on the oval lawn, only this time it was just us—Peter, Bettine, and me. *Well, Alpha Cat was there, too.* Yes, our terrace was a very happy place. The sun set…the moon rose…the angels opened their windows in the sky, and the frogs and crickets sang…and all along, the waterfalls played. *This was my realm.*

A frequent guest was a very attractive lady who wasn't a member of our community, but she had an aura about her. She wore beautiful dresses. Her name was Jackie. Sometimes, she brought her granddaughter, who had a rather unusual name…Kashian. One afternoon when Kashian was riding Angelo in the stable field, she had a fall. I could see she was hurt, so I ran to comfort her. I sat beside her. The others gathered around. After a while, a van came with flashing lights, and they took Kashian away. I was very glad when later that night I heard Peter and Bettine talking about her.

"Thank goodness, she's not hurt…nothing broken," Bettine said

"Wasn't it interesting how Orbit ran to her and wouldn't leave her side until the ambulance came?" Peter noted.

That's my task. I'm here to help people.

A healer, who'd helped Kashian a lot, came to the house. Sometimes, he would work on Kashian, Jackie, and even Bettine and Peter. He usually worked on them downstairs in the big guestroom. On one occasion, Peter's back was bothering him, and this man said he could help him. I was upstairs in the great-room with Bettine and Jackie. We heard Peter scream. I raced down the stairs, through the den, and bounded up on the bed in the guestroom to protect Peter. The man looked startled. I growled at him. Peter was obviously in pain. I could feel it as he held my head. After Peter was hurt, even if the man didn't mean to hurt him, I just couldn't trust him. When he came to our house, I barked and growled, although in all fairness, he sometimes won me over by bringng me tasty steak.

One of the most beautiful occasions was when Peter and Bettine had a group of friends to dine on a balmy June evening. It seemed to be extra special. Laura came and prepared their dinner, and when the guests arrived, they were all dressed up in their best. After they sat down, I took my customary place near where Bettine was sitting. Peter took up one of those crystal glasses, looked at Bettine and said, "Today, we have been married ten years. Happy Anniversary!" And he kissed her. Everyone applauded. The evening was warm, and they all sat there long after the sun set and the moon came up. Their faces glowed in the light of the oil lamps, and then, of course, Bettine played her flutes for them… and guess what…I sang!

I didn't always sing, though. I had to feel that it was right to sing. I had to concentrate on the music. On one occasion, Bettine and Peter drove me to a concert in Marshfield. I discovered that there are many Amish farms along the road from Diggins to Marshfield. We passed several buggies, and I barked fiercely at them. However, I couldn't help noticing the little Amish children, sitting face-out from the back of the buggies, wearing round, straw hats. I don't care for the Amish as I've explained. I believe they consider us animals inferior. Joanne once suggested to Peter and Bettine that it has something to do with the way they look at the Bible. Apparently in this Bible—some collection of holy books for humans—Joanne said, "It is written that God created humans after he created the flora and us animals, so we could be used by the humans, who are supposedly made in God's image." *We are not in God's image?* To me this is rigid thinking, but Joanne said, "The Amish really believe this." *No wonder they treat us the way they do. But, their children…they don't seem so rigid. They might still see everything as one, like me.*

Anyway, I was thinking all these things, when we arrived in Marshfield at a puppet theater—the Jubilee Theater. Bettine set everything up with Peter for her concert. I knew she would try and get me to sing for the people at the end of her concert, and I watched as the people started to come. They were curious to see me, and some of them petted me. My mind, however, was still on the Amish. When the time came, and Peter released me, I started to make my way up to the stage, but I couldn't concentrate on the high-pitched little flute. Instead, I just sat down on the stage and started to clean myself in that place that humans seem to think is private.

CHAPTER EIGHT

Unity Church

"In some places, you just have to obey the rules."

APPARENTLY, THAT SPEAKER, WHO SPOKE to our people just after that "Nine-Eleven" event, seemed to be popular among our community members. According to Bettine, he was famous for three books he had written titled, *Conversations with God*. I find it difficult to see how one can have a conversation with God. This seems to be where the humans have got it wrong. They think everything is about them, including their God. Peter once said: "Nothing exists in our perception except through Divine light." *Can you have a conversation with Divine light? You can feel it...but can you talk to it?*

One day, before Bettine was to play a concert in Springfield, they took me with them. We went into an interesting building with a pointed ceiling rather like we had at Alpha Meadows, and there were windows all down the sides. One side, the windows looked out onto a garden, and on the other side to grass and trees. The room was dark, and full of rows of heavy wooden seats. Unusual lanterns hung from the ceiling. At one end, there was a platform like a stage. I had to sit with Peter at the back, while Bettine played her flutes among a small band of musicians sitting up there. Peter had me on a leash. They hardly ever tied me to a leash.

During a break, Bettine came back to us. "Orbit, you must be very good," she said quietly. "I know these benches are made of wood, but don't think they are trees."

I looked at Peter.

"I'll take him out and make sure he pees on the real trees," he said, and we went out of a side door onto the grass where I found trees.

"Now, you mustn't pee in the church," Peter said while I was relieving myself.

The church…what's a church. This building must be a church. I remembered there was a church the other side of Johnny's field…Johnny called it Caldwell Chapel.

"This is where people worship God," Peter explained.

Yeah! Talk to God! You know, if we're all one, we're all the same…dogs, cats, flowers and trees, rocks and ponds…even smelly armadillos—all one, and only defined in our perception of each other's form by light. I thought that was pretty neat.

The next day, we came back to the church in the morning. Many of the people from our community were there. Dick sat next to us. Leone and Maryloulena came. But, I couldn't see Gabriel. Many other people whom I'd never seen before were there, too. There was a lot of singing. Some man talked for a long time that was rather boring. There was a lot of talk about light, and someone or something called, Christ. Then Bettine was announced, and she walked up with her gold flute and played. I observed the people's faces. They were listening to every note. After that, there was more talk, and someone made an extraordinary sound by rubbing a stick around the rim of a glass bowl. Apart from Bettine's music, the best moment for me was when the pianist started to play a catchy little tune. All these children, led by three or four pretty girls, walked in singing, "I am walking in the light, in the light, in the light; I am walking in the light, in the light of God." And yes, there in their midst was Gabriel. They all stood on the stage and repeated something with the girls. Gabriel didn't open his mouth, however. He just smiled at Maryloulena.

When the children had finished, everyone stood up, holding hands as they sang some song all about peace on earth. When it was over, they started chattering. Many of the children came up to me and patted my head. I'd never seen so many children. We didn't see a lot of children at Alpha Meadows. I liked it when they patted me on the head. *I am walking in the light, in the light, in the light; I am walking in the light, in the light of God. These children are onto something.*

"What's his name?" a little girl asked.

"Orbit," Peter replied.

I looked at the girl, my tongue hanging out. She smiled at me. "Orbit," she repeated, putting her arms around my neck.

After this church meeting, I went with Peter and Bettine somewhere in the Explorer. They told me to "be a good doggie," and then went inside this building with little flags hanging down over the entrance that had funny writing on them—apparently, Japanese. I slept on the back seat of the car until they came out. Bettine put down a white box for me with rice and some vegetables covered in a tasty sauce. I quickly ate the contents.

"So, Orby, you like Japanese?" Bettine said.

I licked the sides of my jaw with my tongue. *Yes.*

Then we went back to the church again. They called it, Unity Church. The musicians were there, and Bettine went over a few things with them. Peter and I sat at the back as we had in the morning, while many of the same people there in the morning returned for Bettine's concert. I noticed a plant that looked like a small tree by the stage. I felt some urge to mark it and started walking toward it. Just before I reached it, I saw Bettine glaring at me. I turned around and went back to Peter.

When the church was full, Bettine came to us and said, "Later, I'm going to ask you to sing." I looked up at her, and then put my head down on my crossed paws.

A lady stood up and said something from the stage, and Bettine started to play her flute as she walked up the path between the rows of wooden seats. When she reached the stage, the band started to play with her, and the concert began. I recognized most of the music, and sometimes, when Bettine was talking in between tunes, there was laughter. Finally, she picked up the little flute. Peter took off my leash. *Oh, so now I'm to sing.* As Bettine began to play, I started to walk between the rows, stopping and looking up at the faces of the people. That seemed to please them. Finally, I reached Bettine. She started to play my tunes, very fast. The sound penetrated my ears, and I threw back my head and started to howl the notes. I sang. As usual, at the end, there was both laughter and applause. Bettine looked very happy and threw out her hand in a gesture to me.

I stood at the table after the concert where so many people bought recordings of her music. They all patted me on my head, and they all now knew my name. These were the Unity people, and a lot of them came to visit us at Alpha Meadows. Kashian's grandmother, Jackie, was among these Unity people. Some, like Jackie, came to those dinner parties.

Often, we had thunderstorms that reverberated down our valley. Thunder scared me, but one night was particularly dramatic. This time, I think everyone was frightened. Brian, carrying a yellow talking-box, and Rajah, Joanne, along with Job and Susan, all came up to our house from the trailer. "Now we can test out the storm shelter," Brian said. "They're forecasting tornadoes." *Tornadoes?* I figured tornadoes must be even worse storms than the thunder and lightning.

The rain was slashing down as a truck drove up. A bedraggled Bear jumped out, followed by Joy, wrapped in a blanket, her hair completely soaked. Michael followed. "The tent just collapsed on us," he said.

Bear whimpered in the mud room, while Joy tried to dry him with a towel. There was a terrific crack of thunder, and through the great-room windows the night sky turned silver, as above us, yellow forks made patterns in the menacing sky.

"Everyone downstairs!" Brian yelled.

Bettine grabbed me. "You, too, Orbit."

"Let me get Alpha from upstairs," Peter said.

We made our way into the back of the basement where there were always noises from pumps and furnaces, but this night, it seemed like a quiet haven somewhat muted in contrast with the almost continuous thunder outside. It was a while, however, before Brian joined us. Alpha ran toward the guest bedroom door when Brian opened it. "Don't let Alpha escape?" Peter yelled

"There's a hook at Ozark and it's heading our way," Brian said, still clutching the yellow talking-box.

"What about the horses, the donkey, and Harry Trotter?" Bettine asked.

"Oh, they'll be all right unless we get a direct hit."

A strange smell of wet clothing filled the fug of the furnace room as we all huddled together. I nuzzled between Joanne and Bettine. We stayed there for some time. The talking-box droned on in a monotonous voice.

"No touch down," Brian said at length. From his tone of voice he seemed disappointed. "I'm going back up."

I followed with Peter and Bettine. There was still thunder, but it seemed farther away and there were fewer of those yellow, forked streaks in the sky—just flashes. And then, eventually, dark silence, until the moon emerged from the clouds.

Brian and Joanne left with Susan and Job, but Michael and Joy stayed downstairs, sleeping with Bear on the big bed in the guestroom. I scratched on the glass door, and Bettine let me out on the upper deck. I could see the horses and Dominique in the moonlight, and, yes, Angelo had his neck over the fence into Harry Trotter's pen. It seemed that all was well.

Not long after that bad storm, Bettine and Peter took me into Springfield. We went to this wonderful place they called, Petsmart. I liked it there as there were lots of other dogs, although I had to wear a leash—a rather flimsy leash. Oh boy! Were the smells good in that place! There were dogs of every size, and we all seemed to get along very well, but of course, we were in the presence of our owners. Eventually, we stopped in an area where there were all sorts of baskets and dog houses. "Now, Orbit, you have to choose a kennel," Bettine said. "We want you to have a house in case there are bad storms when we're away." I looked up at her, quizzically. *Most these houses are way too small for me.* But, there was one…much bigger than all the others. I went up to it and sniffed around. I could tell that many dogs had walked in and out of it. I sauntered in. *Roomy…I could fit in this one.* I looked out from the entrance.

"I think this one will work for him," Peter said.

Bettine laughed. "Of course, he's picked way the most expensive kennel."

"So you like this one?" she said to me.

I walked out and wagged my tail.

"Well, I suppose we'd better buy this kennel for you. You chose it, Orby."

A salesman marked it sold.

"We'll never get that into our car," Peter said.

"We can hold it until you can pick it up, sir. Just take this ticket to the cashier up front."

We drove home without my new house, but the next day, Clive delivered it in his blue truck. He then built a platform for the kennel right beside our house and overlooking the oval lawn.

My house. I looked at the kennel proudly. But you know what, I never really used it. I preferred to lie in the shade under the Explorer, or out on the oval lawn when the shadows came, just like I always had. *Maybe, if there is a bad storm, I might use it, but I would prefer to be in the mud room.*

After Bettine came home from her tours, she often performed at the Unity church, and nobody seemed to mind if I sat with Peter during their services. Everybody at Unity got to know who I was. Then one day, the lady who seemed to be in charge at Unity, Sue Baggett, came to Alpha Meadows for lunch. Her daughter came with her. They were both very beautiful—filled with light.

I've always seen radiance around people, but I also see light around flowers and leaves. There's lots of radiance in Peter's garden. The children's song reverberated in my head: *"I am walking in the light, in the light, in the light; I am walking in the light, in the light of God." What blocks humans from seeing this light all the time? I see it. The flowers and trees, the clouds, the sun and the moon…they have it all the time. They're better teachers than some human God. Why are the humans so hung up on their God?*

When Bettine took me to the Unity church, I wanted to give my light to all the new people whom I met. But, before we went into the place where they had the music and they sang, I usually made my way into Sue Baggett's office. There was an interesting musty smell in there, but I loved this lady. Sometimes, when I sat there before the service, she gave me cookies. Then she would get up from her desk and say, "Okay, Orbit, it's time to go," and she would put her hand on my head. I could feel the energy move between us. Inspired, I then joined Peter and Bettine and took my place among the people. I knew my task. *Spread light.*

Another lady came to stay with us. She was very slim, dark-haired, and smelled like the roses in Peter's garden. I took an immediate liking to her. It seemed that she was to play a concert with Bettine and they spent a lot of time making music together—the lady playing on the big instrument they called, the Steinway, and Bettine with her flutes. It was rare that anyone played the Steinway; so I didn't hear it very often. I loved the reverberating sounds that came from it—deep tones. Up to this point, I had just considered it to be a large, odd-shaped table in the great-room, but when the lady played, I ran from wherever I was, as I liked to get really close to this Steinway. I couldn't work out where the sound was coming from, but it filled the room. I also just wanted to be near this special lady.

"I think Orbit likes you," Bettine said to the pianist.

Bettine looked at me: "You like the Piano Princess?"

Piano Princess. Yes, I like this Piano Princess. I love this Piano Princess. I sniffed her perfume. *Roses!*

Of course, I loved Bettine...I loved Joanne...I loved Peter. These were my people; but there was something about this Piano Princess that was different for me. I wanted to be close to her. I really didn't know why. She didn't feed me food. In fact, apart from occasionally patting me on the head, she didn't communicate with me much, but I was drawn to her sweetness—her aroma...and yes, her aura. I was also drawn to the wonderful combination of sounds that reverberated up into the rafters of our great-room when the music of the Steinway blended with the music of the flute. I looked up to the loft. I could see Alpha's curiosity arisen, when she poked her little, gray and white face through the banisters.

The Piano Princess only stayed a couple of days, then she was gone. *Bummer...*I made my way to Alpha's bowl in the kitchen and helped myself to her cat food. But for some time after the Piano Princess left, I felt I was walking in the light, in the light, in the light; I was walking in the light, in the light of God. *These so-called Divine connections, they're strange.*

CHAPTER NINE

Peter and Bettine

"I can feel it so much when my people are sad and suffering."

I LAY ON THE FLOOR as usual, close to Peter and Bettine in the screen porch, wondering whether I would get some chicken. Brian and Joanne had come for dinner. I knew something was wrong. Brian looked different, drawn in to himself, almost sad. Where was *his* light? I looked up at him, but he cast his eyes away. "I'm going to Florida," he said to Bettine, "to work on the book." *What book?* "I'm inspired by what I saw at Findhorn," Brian continued, "now...*they* understand community."

"Brian has a friend who is giving him his beachfront apartment for a few weeks," Joanne explained. "There, he can write."

I looked up at Brian. *He doesn't feel very excited about it. There's more to this. Brian looks crushed.*

"Joanne won't be coming. We need to go our own ways," Brian said. "The Sage Hill Institute could have been the Findhorn of the Midwest."

I raised myself up and put a paw on Brian's lap. At last, I saw him smile, just faintly. Then Bettine gave me a piece of her white chicken meat. We didn't see Brian for a long time after that. He just disappeared.

One time, while Peter and Bettine were traveling and Al and Julie were taking care of me and Alpha, Joanne came by. We went on a walk through the woods just north of Fred's place. Of course, Timo came, too.

Joanne looked at Al. "Finally, you'll be able to build on your lot," she said.

"Yes, I think we picked out the best location."

"And when my house is finished, we'll almost be neighbors," Joanne continued.

Timo ran off into the woods. I chased after him. He suddenly stood still and barked loudly. I joined him. Three deer stood in front of us, their liquid eyes staring straight at us—a mama deer and two baby deer. Then they turned and jumped down into a ravine. Timo continued to bark.

When we came back to the others, they were already at the cabin.

"So, when will Michael and Joy move in?" Al asked.

"As soon as they've finished painting," Joanne said.

Al walked around the half-painted structure. "Will they always have this cabin, or will they eventually have to pull it down and build to the standards of our agreement?" Al asked.

Joanne looked at him. "Eventually, I would think. We want Alpha Meadows North to be a high-quality development. But we can't expect them to stay in their tent through the winter. Remember how it collapsed in that storm."

Timo peed on the timbers. I followed him, but it wasn't just Timo I smelled. I sniffed again. *Bear? Bear's been here. This must be Bear's new place. Yes, Michael, Joy, and Bear, must be coming to live here.*

Some days, Holly went riding with Peter and Bettine. As usual, I followed them as they rode the trails to Joanne's new farm, past the community cabins and through the woods. Between the woods and the farmhouse, there was a beautiful meadow filled with white, lacey blooms, and yellow and purple, daisy-like flowers. The horses often galloped through here, and I would run behind them with my flying ears. On this particular day, when they stopped to rest, the horses were close to Joanne's place.

"I think Joanne's lonely," Bettine suggested.

Holly relaxed the reins and looked down at the ground. "What's happening to us all," she said. "I've heard Job and Susan have split."

"Really?"

"Yes, now that she's giving up the fire station, I think they've decided to go separate ways. I think she's staying in the community cabin, but she's talking about building her own cabin."

There was a deathly silence as they both looked at me. I could see such sadness in Holly's eyes. "Bernadette's leaving, too," she said.

"What?"

"Yes. I think it's just too quiet for her out here. She wants to go back to Springfield."

They started to walk the horses up the rugged track that climbed out of the valley to the road. Many rocks and washed out ravines criss-crossed our path.

A week or two later, I ventured past Laughing Dragons Lodge, hoping Kiri wouldn't see me. She was becoming quite unfriendly toward me. I went on down the hill in the woods until I came to Bear's cabin. Michael and Joy were there, but they seemed to be having some kind of an argument, and at length, Michael stormed out with Bear. *Something's not right with them, either.* Michael and Bear drove away.

The door to the cabin was still open, and I nuzzled my way in. I sniffed the air. There was a funny smell inside. I saw a broken bottle on the floor, the source of the strong vapors. I liked Joy. She still spent many hours working in our garden at Alpha Meadows. She loved our flowers, just like Peter, but in here, she was sitting on an old kitchen chair, crying. I put my head in her lap and looked up at her.

She smiled through her tears. "Orbit," she said, choking. She stroked the top of my head. I put my paw up. *I'm here for you.* Joy let me stay with her for some while. "He drinks, Orbit; he just drinks too much," she said.

When I returned home, Peter was mowing. He was always mowing.

I could tell that there was something else wrong when Bettine came back from a concert cruise to Alaska—some place "up north," she said. Peter spent a lot of time at his computer in the den. He seemed very upset. He was apparently writing a book, too. *Just like Brian. What's happening? Something doesn't feel right. Things* are *different.*

A few weeks later, when Bettine was on another of her tours, Peter also went away for a weekend. He left me with M and M. Actually, I liked M and M. They were always kind to me, and we would all sit watching that big screen. They seemed to still like that pirate movie. By day, however, I ruled my kingdom, or chased the donkey.

Peter seemed happy when he came home. It was dusk, and I was lying in the long evening shadows that fell over the oval lawn. I heard his jeep coming up the drive. I could always tell from the sound if it was his or Bettine's car. I felt relieved to know he was coming home. That night, I climbed on the bed and lay beside him. I wanted to ask him where he'd been, and I knew he sensed my concern.

When Bettine came back from her travels, we would pick her up at the airport. Peter used to leave me in the back of the Explorer, but I knew where I was, and it wasn't a surprise when they came out together. They always looked happy then, illuminated by the fuzzy light of the big overhead parking lamps. Peter would let me out, and I could smell Bettine. I would roll on the ground and wag my tail and show her how much I loved her, and how much we had both missed her, while Peter put her luggage in the car. I would sit with Bettine all the way home, my head nuzzling her lap, while she stroked my head. Sometimes, we stopped on the way home, and Bettine bought me summer sausage. At the house, Peter always had a little dinner prepared for Bettine that he lovingly served, accompanied by a bottle of wine. There were still good times, but something *was* different.

Things seemed wrong elsewhere in our world. Kiri spent a lot of time away from Fred. The good thing about that was Fred used to invite me in to Laughing Dragons Lodge to watch those moving pictures on his big screen. However, I could easily sense that Fred was lonely, and that he felt something was wrong. Then there was Joy. She left the little cabin in the woods. She told Peter one day, as they were talking in the garden, that she had bought a field somewhere on Dillon Road—the road to Johnny's place. Michael was gone. When I went up to the community cabins, I saw Susan in her new place. It wasn't far from Clive's cabin, but she lived there alone. Job was not there for her anymore. Everybody seemed more stressed than they had been in the early community days. And then Al and Julie left. Bettine said they decided to move to some place called Asheville, in the Carolinas—a long way from us. Of course, they took my friend Timo with them. *What's happening?* I kept repeating to myself. *What's happening to our world?*

Bettine and Peter seemed to argue a lot at this time. They were stressed out. I could feel it. They paid less attention to me. I overheard them talk about money.

"How are we going to be able to keep this place going if everyone in the community seems to be moving away, and there are no more courses? You have no money. Why can't you sell your books? It's always me. I have to keep everything going. I work non-stop, and it's never enough!"

I hated it when they started yelling at each other, and I nuzzled them with my nose, letting them know that this was not cool. It worked. I made them laugh, and they gave each other a healing hug; but it never used to be like this.

When Bettine was traveling, I often snuggled up to Peter on the bed. "Orbit," he said one night. "What can I do? I'm losing Bettine. She's not always traveling alone, you know. She's spending too much time with these other people." I patted Peter with my paw and looked into his eyes. *What people?*

In between, however, there were happy times on the terrace. We had lots of dinner parties out there. There were less courses now, but different groups came to these dinners, and Peter spent hours preparing the table for them. Peter dressed up in this fancy red vest and black trousers, and waited on them. Sometimes, Bettine played flute for them. Several times, Laura came and prepared the food. I used to sit on the terrace and listen to the frogs and crickets. If I heard the munching sound of advancing armadillos, I ran off to chase them. I liked showing off to our guests that this was my kingdom. I loved to hear the exclamations of these guests, when they walked out on our terrace and saw the bevy of beauty all around them.

Later, in the fall, another group of people came to our house for a writing conference. They were interesting people and all made a big fuss of me. It seemed like the good days again. But, it didn't last. It was the same old story. "Why don't we make any money from these events?"

Bettine said after the people had left. "At least, when we had the courses, we made a little money from the guesthouse and teaching fees."

They're talking about money again.

Bettine beat her fist against her desk. "And now, after this conference," she shouted, "Kiri doesn't even want us to use Laughing Dragons Lodge anymore!"

"No more guests…it's as if we built all this for nothing," Peter said. "Why do they only want the courses in Florida now?"

"How do I know?… Money!" Bettine yelled. "It's always about money! We've poured everything into this place, and now we're running out of money! Don't they understand? Soon, there will be nothing left. How can we afford to keep this huge place without the courses? And, why do you pay Joy in the garden? Do we really need all this garden?"

I saw Peter look away and roll his eyes.

Stop this! Remember how you held hands on the horses?

Soon after this, Bettine left on another long tour. I spent many nights on the bed with Peter. I could sense his sadness. He would hold me as if asking me to comfort him. I was always there for him. Sometimes, he would wake up, calling out Bettine's name, "Bettine…Come home, Bettine."

One Sunday, when Bettine was home, we all went to the Unity church. Bettine played her flutes during the service, and Peter was introduced, and got up and spoke for a long time about some Mary Magdalene. It turned out that this Mary was a friend of a man named Jesus, who was mentioned occasionally in the Unity church as the Christ. Peter suggested this Jesus and Mary Magdalene might have had a son, and that many things might have been quite different. *Is that important? So what! Besides, Peter said these were all people who lived a long time ago. Not people we know.* The people at Unity listened intently, however. Peter's talk was long, and I could sense that he was speaking very passionately. This talking time in the service, however, is a good time to snooze. I prefer it when that bowl reverberates, or when the children come in singing that song, *I am walking in the light.* I noticed Gabriel wasn't among these children any more. Maryloulena didn't seem to come to the Unity church much now. At the end, however, everyone stood up as usual, holding hands and swaying as they sang that peace song. *Well, this means it's getting closer to rice time.* Then, of course, all the children came by to pet me. *Well, if it makes them happy, that's my task.*

Peter and Bettine had books and CDs at a table in the foyer. I stood there as people looked them over. Some bought books, and many bought CDs. Peter and Bettine's friend, Jackie, also stood there with us.

"I'm fascinated by Mary Magdalene," a young woman said, while looking at the back cover of one of Peter's books.

The woman bought the book, and Peter signed it.

"Who shall I say it's for?" he asked.

"Nanette."

Jackie came with us to the rice restaurant. In the car, she asked Peter what he thought of *The Da Vinci Code.*

Another book I suppose…

"Well, it's certainly got a lot of publicity," Peter answered.

"But, in *The Da Vinci Code*, Jesus has a child with Mary Magdalene," Jackie said. "I think you should read this book."

We arrived at the restaurant. I settled down to nap until they all came out with my rice.

Shortly after that, Bettine left for yet another tour. Peter seemed sad. I tried to comfort him at night when I climbed up on the bed. Then, for about four days, Peter started reading a book. He read it day and long into the night. It was a fat book, and there was gold writing on the cover. It was very late when we went upstairs.

"I'm sorry, Orby," he said as he cuddled up to me. He'd started calling me Orby in his loneliness. I sort of liked it. It was bonding. "I had to get this book finished. Tomorrow, I have to talk about it. Our friend, Jackie, has got me involved in some discussion panel about this book, *The Da Vinci Code.*"

So what! Let's sleep. It's funny, I can actually hear myself snoring when I sleep on the bed. Of course, I don't really sleep…I rest…my eyes are always half open.

One evening, Peter went into Springfield and left me in the house. Of course, this was a great opportunity for me to get up on the sofa. I knew I wasn't supposed to be there, but who would ever know? *Not taking me with him. What next?* I looked up from my comfortable place. There was Alpha Cat stretched out between the banisters with one paw in the air. *Why does she never fall from there? It would scare me.* Once again, it reminded me of the Amish people, when they were building our house. *I guess they did do a good job. Maybe, they're not so bad after all.*

However, while Bettine was away, Peter and I had a great day with Joanne's mother and father at Finley Farms. There was plenty of food that became lots of tidbits, and they called it, Thanksgiving. Again, the smell emanating from the kitchen was delicious—a sweet mix of spices, fruits, and roasted meat. It was warm and inviting, with steaming saucepans on the stovetop and hidden pans telling me there was meat in the oven. All the community people, who were still around, came. Peter and Bettine never made much of this Thanksgiving at Alpha Meadows, but it seemed to be a huge event for Joanne's family. I liked it. I got turkey rather than chicken. Actually, turkey tasted even better than chicken.

Before Bettine came home, however, Peter often went into town and didn't come back until late at night, even early the next morning. I was alone a lot, and sometimes, I felt uncomfortable in the house, not being able to go out and pee. I was relieved when Peter prepared the house again, and we went together to the airport. I knew Bettine was coming home.

Peter seemed really pleased to see Bettine. *I wish she didn't have to go away so much. I like it when we are all together.* The next three weeks were a very happy time. Peter put this huge fir-tree up in the great-room, like he did every year. It had lots of twinkling lights among its branches, illuminating colored balls. A growing number of parcels spread around it. In the evenings, the three of us sat close to the log fire in the big chimney-piece, and Peter and Bettine sipped on wine from those crystal glasses. This was living, and I happily stretched out beside them, toasting myself. But, I heard mention of "Mexico," and then, the suitcases came out again...*bummer!*

The evening before they left, they exchanged many of the parcels. They even thanked me for gifts that I knew nothing about. I doubt, the horses, Harry Trotter, or Alpha, knew about them either, but we all seemed to have gifts for Peter and Bettine, and there were gifts for me too—summer sausage, tasty toy bones, and a book that said: *When good dogs do bad things.* Sometimes, I still felt the shame of attacking Harry Trotter's ears. This book, however, seemed to make them laugh. It was good to see them happy. There was less talk about money.

At Christmas, Bettine and Peter both went away on that Mexican concert cruise, and on the way to the airport, they took me to this big house near Springfield, where I stayed with Laura Lucey. I liked Laura. She was always cooking, and she used to feed me all sorts of tidbits. But she confided in me. "Orbit," she said, as I sat beside her in the kitchen, "Help me. My husband wants a divorce."

What's a divorce?

She started to cry.

A divorce must be something bad. I put my paw up on her lap. I just looked at her until she smiled and hugged me.

Then it started to snow. Laura and I went out together and played. We became constant companions, and I felt that somehow I *was* helping her. But Laura looked very sad when Peter and Bettine came to fetch me on their return from that Mexico place. I watched her as we drove away in the Explorer. *Sometimes, it's hard to understand humans. Two people, who seem to love each other, all of a sudden hate each other. Divorce...We dogs love everybody unless they threaten us, and that goes for other dogs as well as humans.*

That winter, things were not good. Bettine spent a lot of time on the computer in her small office. I would sit close to her. But, sometimes she closed the door, and even I could not be with her. I heard her frequently talking on the phone as I scratched at the far side. Bettine cried often... Peter, too. Money frequently came up again. *Why do the humans always worry so much about money? I know they have to buy all of us animals food, but the horses and donkey eat grass or hay, which is there anyway... well, perhaps they have to buy the hay. Alpha and I can't cost much. Harry Trotter eats mostly stale dog food and kitchen leftovers. Somehow, we will all survive harder times if we just keep together and keep loving each other. If humans will only realize that no matter what, love and closeness is the most important stuff in life. We dogs and animals know this.*

Beautiful yellow bushes start to bloom all over Alpha Meadows every spring. Peter calls them, forsythia. Complimenting them, huge pink flowers bloom on other bushes, taller than the forsythia…apparently, magnolias. Small trees also blossom in pink, purple, and white, in many places adjacent to the forsythia and magnolias…crab apples. *Funny names.* The real apple trees behind the big deer fence that didn't keep any of us animals out, also burst into a mass of blush blossoms this time of the year. Daffodils and tulips are up in the flower gardens, and yellow and purple pansies fill all the terrace tubs and deck containers. Spring is my favorite season. Everything suddenly comes to life all at about the same time. White clouds scurry across our sky, and the fresh green grass looks verdant in its new growth.

But, spring that year quickly turned into the summer of hell. Another writer's conference was held at our house. Some of the people were there from the year before, but among the new faces, was a tall, young lady with long, blonde hair, attending with a girlfriend of hers from St. Louis. They stayed down at the guesthouse, but Peter spent a lot of time with them. He seemed to know them. Apparently, they had met at that discussion on *The Da Vinci Code*. I sensed some strange chemistry between this girl and Peter, and I saw that Bettine felt this, too. The girl's name was Marie, and although she was very sweet to me, and I could tell she liked animals, I knew something was really not right here when Bettine became very quiet—sad looking.

After this conference, things got really bad. One day, Peter came home quite late, and he and Bettine started shouting at each other. Then I heard that word again. Peter said, "I want a divorce." I thought of Laura when she talked to me in the kitchen at her house. *Divorce…* Bettine burst into tears and cried violently, "No! I don't want that!" She broke down. I tried to run to her and comfort her. She buried her face in my fur, and I could feel the damp of her tears reach my flesh.

Later, Holly came by. Bettine, Peter, and Holly, sat on the big sofa for a while, and talked intensely, while I lay at their feet, licking my paws. After much discussion, it seemed that Holly advised Bettine to let Peter go. So, after Holly left, his suitcases came out. He silently packed clothes, then carried the suitcases downstairs. I lay by the front door. I didn't want him to leave. I didn't want to let him out. He knelt down beside me.

He was crying, and wiped his wet tears on my fur. "Goodbye, Orby," he said, chokingly. "I love you. Take great care of Bettine. We both love you, Orby!" Then, audibly sobbing, he hugged and kissed Bettine. I thought I heard him say, "I love you, too," before he carried the suitcases out to his jeep.

Bettine and I stood at the front door as he drove off. The jeep made a roaring noise as it raced down the driveway and away from us. When we came back in, I felt terrible. Bettine cried so much. I tried to comfort her. But then, I went outside and sat in the driveway waiting, hoping for Peter to return. The moon rose, and I sat there and looked out all night until dawn broke. I sat on the oval lawn all day, waiting…I only went back in to comfort Bettine, and she tried to comfort me. "We'll get through this," she said gently, but I knew she was hurting as much as me. We held each other, and yet we knew somehow that Peter wasn't coming back. I kept up my vigil for about a week, sitting on the oval lawn all day, and comforting Bettine as best I could all night. Bettine often opened a bottle of wine and drank the whole bottle. Probably, she tried to numb her pain and loneliness that way. I hated the smell of the alcohol. It reminded me of that sad day when Michael and Bear left Joy in that cabin below Laughing Dragons Lodge. When Bettine cried, both Alpha and I tried to comfort her. In the bed, with that vista of all the night stars, I lay next to her, and Alpha on the other side or on top of her. Alpha woke her up many times, just to check if she was still breathing. Finally, Bettine started to laugh, "Alpha, I'm still alive, you don't have to wake me up and check five times a night." She hugged us both. *This is our task. We must hold Bettine in our love.*

CHAPTER TEN

What's Going On?

"To be or not to be…Live in the moment"

THE GRASS BEGAN TO GROW. My oval lawn lost its stripes. The flowers in the containers started to wilt. Bettine must have noticed. She pulled out the hose and watered them. They revived, but the hose lay all over the terrace like a long snake. I remember seeing a black snake on the lawn below the terrace gardens once…it stretched out from our flowerbeds all the way down to the woods. I didn't often see snakes, but I was wary of them when I did. Anyway, that's sort of what this hose looked like…not neatly coiled up by the faucet as it had been after Peter watered. Inside, the kitchen counter was cluttered—dishes and glasses were in the sink, pots and pans never left the stove. The candles on the dining table burned down until wax spilled over the candlesticks. Papers started to pile up on the table. In the great-room, cushions found their way to the floor and stayed there. *It's not like it was when Peter was here. The place feels different.*

Then two people came by to visit. Bettine showed them around. They had white hair, although they were not that old. I think I had seen them at the Unity church. I walked with them all over the property. The man's name was Leonard, and the lady's, Petra. We stopped for a long time in the orchard. The apple trees made a big impression on Leonard. I could tell how much they had grown, even since that time that Peter had tried to keep me in the orchard after the incident with Harry Trotter.

"How are you going to market these apples?" Leonard asked.

"My husband used to sell them to organic stores like Mama Jean's," Bettine said, "but there are so many of them."

"I could get people to pick them," Leonard said. "I know places I could sell those. They'd sell very well in the farmers' markets. More people should be growing organic apples."

"You can do what you like with them. Holly and M and M usually take some."

Leonard raised his bushy white brows. "Neighbors?"

"Yes. M and M live in the house just down the hill there, and Holly is our neighbor to the south."

Trail's place.

A few days later, the suitcases came out. Leonard and Petra returned. *Now I'm going to be left with strangers.* And, I was right.

Bettine hugged me for a long time. Then, she went to the fridge and cut me a couple of pieces of summer sausage. "Leonard and Petra are going to take care of you and Alpha while I'm gone. Be nice to them," she said, holding out the summer sausage. I took the two pieces and swallowed them whole.

Leonard put Bettine's suitcases into his truck. Petra held me at the front door as Bettine, with tears in her eyes, hugged me one more time before she got in. They drove away. Petra let me out on the oval lawn. Our place suddenly went very quiet. I felt as if all the joy of my kingdom was gone.

I was still outside when Leonard's truck returned, but Bettine was gone. Leonard walked over to me, and patted my back. "Come on in, Orbit. Let's get your food," he said. I wasn't hungry, but I followed him into the kitchen. Petra was boiling a kettle. Alpha was eating her cat food. *Well, maybe I will have a little of her food. I like her food.* And as soon as she left her dish, I cleaned it out with two or three licks of my tongue.

I don't know how long Bettine was gone, but it seemed forever without Peter being there. The grass continued to grow, so I started to make trails through it. But, eventually, I heard the familiar sound from up by the garden shed beside the windmill. Leonard had started up the big, red lawn mower. He didn't cut much with it, however, just my oval lawn and a swath of grass all around the gardens and up to the terrace. There was lots of cut grass left on the ground after the mowing, and in time it turned smelly and brown…quite interesting, actually, but it attracted flies and gnats. Leonard also started to pick apples in the orchard. I went with him and sat in the shade of the trees as he picked away. "Be careful of those wasps," Leonard said. I looked at the yellow, bee-like creatures that were buzzing around some of the more rotten apples lying on the ground. Then, one day, Clive came by and climbed up to the top of the windmill to feed it something to stop it squeaking. Leonard stood at the bottom, asking all sorts of questions, but I didn't understand their windmill speak, except that I heard the Amish mentioned a few times. *Oh well, Leonard always lets me walk with him, and Petra always smiles at me…I suppose life's not all that bad. But, I do wish Bettine would come home.*

Eventually, Bettine did come home. Leonard and Petra left. I immediately felt Bettine's light and love, and I started to sleep on the bed again.

Not long after that, Leonard and Petra came back to live in our guesthouse that had been empty ever since Al and Julie left. Peter always kept containers on the decks, billowing over with plants just like the one's on our terrace, but they hadn't been watered, and now the plants were all dead. Leonard used to pat my back, and he always talked to me, so I was quite glad he had come to live with us. He had a kind of earthy smell that I liked, too. Leonard spent a lot of time planting vegetables and tomatoes in Peter's big flowerbeds. Actually, the flowerbeds were rapidly growing over with weeds, except in those areas. Leonard also put sprinklers on stands to water the tomatoes, chard, and peppers, he planted. I could have told him the water pressure wasn't going to be strong enough, because I knew Peter had tried that from time to time. Peter always watered everything by hand, dragging out that long hose and then neatly coiling it up again afterwards—the one that now looked like a snake.

I became very astute at recognizing the sound of cars—the way their engine's revved, or the type of sound certain tires made on the gravel roads. I knew when M and M turned into our driveway. I could tell if it was Bettine's Explorer coming up the hill below our guesthouse. I knew the sound of Leonard's truck. I also knew if it was something like the propane tank man's truck, turning off the road into our drive. I heard it coming up the hill. Up in a bound, I was halfway to meet it, when in a swirl of dust the tanker turned the corner in front of Laughing Dragons' Lodge. I stood in front of the orchard, barking for all I was worth until the vehicle reached me, then I chased alongside until it stopped at our house. The man looked down at me from his high cab, and I pretended to be fierce when I looked back up at him. But, he was used to me. Eventually, he opened his door and climbed down. He gave me a cookie. The game was over. I let him do his tanker business, and I returned to my customary position on the oval lawn.

I spent hours lying on the grass, with the buzzing of summer insects around me. But, once in a while, if Dominique came near the adjacent paddock fence, I would get up and chase him away. Amadeus and Angelo liked to splash in the hilltop pond where all those white water lilies grew. On a hot summer's day, I could understand that. Sometimes, after chasing Dominique away, I went into the pond to cool myself down. There was an earthy smell to the water that clung to my underbelly and infiltrated deep within my paws as they wriggled in the muddy bottom. It felt sooooo good.

On a particularly warm day, I had just climbed out of the pond, when I heard the sound of a car turning into the drive. *Can it be….?* I shook myself, muddy droplets flying. I saw the cloud of dust at Laughing Dragons' corner. *I'm sure it is…!* I clambered through the post and rail fence and ran for all I was worth. Beside the orchard, we met…the blue jeep slowed down as I stood in the roadway. I went up to it, sniffed at the front tire, and looked up to see Peter smiling down from the open window.

"Oh…Orbit!" he choked. "Orbit! I love you, Orbit!" He opened the door, and I put up my muddy paws and licked his face. Peter hugged me for all he was worth. "I'm coming home," he whispered, fluffing my ears, "home to you and my beloved Bettine!"

I climbed up into the back seat of the jeep. Together, we drove up to the house. Before we had even got out of the car, Bettine opened the front door. "I love you. I want to come home," was all Peter said. And when

Bettine saw me sitting up in the back seat, she smiled—a light-filled, radiant smile.

That night, I climbed up on the bed and lay between them. I was so very, very happy. I rolled over and thrust back my head on the pillows, looking alternately into their loving eyes. I could hear Alpha, too, purring loudly. Moonlight streamed in through the big windows, and all the angel-stars blinked in harmony.

For a few days, there were dinners on the terrace with steak and chicken. Sometimes, Leonard and Petra joined us. Often, Peter and Bettine danced to the French lady's singing. The bullfrogs seemed to bellow deeper, and the crickets and tree frogs sang so high that I was tempted to howl. Slowly, order came back to the house. The long black snake of the hose became coiled again, and Peter cut the grass…all the grass. But, then the day came when the suitcases re-appeared. Bettine tried to pack them, but Alpha kept sitting in them. It was as if Alpha knew something. She didn't want Bettine to go away. I sniffed at Alpha in the suitcase. "It's all right, Bettine has to go away, but Peter's here now. We'll guard the house until she comes back."

Bettine looked at Peter. "They love us so much," she said. Then she held up a shaggy sweater. "For Iceland! I wish you could come with me. I love Iceland, and we could ride those ponies together."

We followed the old routine. Peter drove us to the airport in the Explorer. I came out onto the curb to meet the friendly security officer. He patted me on the head and said my name. Bettine beckoned for me to get back in the car. She hugged me. "Be a good boy," she said, tears welling in her eyes. "Peter will be with you." Peter then drove us to the parking lot, and left me to snooze as he went back to the terminal. Some time passed before he returned, alone, without Bettine. *She's travelling again, playing her flutes to feed Alpha and me.* Silently, we drove back to Alpha Meadows. The house, the garden, it all seemed very quiet again, except for the persistent buzzing of pesky flies.

In the evening, I started to play the Orbit game with Peter, just like old times. As soon as the sun set, if I was not already in the house, I would run off and wait for him to find me. When he came looking, I would run off farther until I knew he would have to come after me in the car. I had run down to M and M's house. Peter stopped the Explorer and got out, calling for me as he always did. He walked down to Holly's house thinking I might be there, but in his haste, he left the door of the car open. I jumped in and lay down on the back seat. When Peter returned, I didn't reveal to him I was there. He drove all over the community property looking for me. Finally, after about half an hour, I put my paw up between the front seats and gave a little bark, "Game's over."

Peter was startled, but then he began to laugh. "Oh, Orbit," he said, "you really played the Orbit Game well tonight. You've been in here all the time?"

I fooled you. Now, let's go home. I win!

Some days, Peter told me he had to work on the garden at the park in Springfield. Peter rubbed my ears each time before he left. When he came back in the evening, he usually took me into Seymour, where he ate Chinese food at a place called, the Twin Dragons. Afterward, he would bring me a doggie bag full of my favorite rice and sweet and sour chicken in a tasty sauce. I always ate it up before getting back in the car, where on our short journey home, I licked the stickiness from around my mouth and nose.

One evening, while Bettine was in Iceland, when Peter came back from Springfield, he looked very strange…distant, not exactly sad, but definitely confused. He told me many times how much he loved me. *Something's wrong. What's going on?* He was restless. He didn't sleep much. For a while, in the middle of the night, we sat together on the deck, looking over the horse paddock in the moonlight. I could see Amadeus, Angelo, and that irritating Dominique, lapping at the pond where the white water lilies seemed to reflect the luminosity of the night sky. I could hear armadillos munching and digging in the oval lawn. Usually, that really annoyed Peter. He would go out and chase them. But, this night, he didn't seem to hear them. He was somewhere else, far away, and I thought he was crying. "I'm so sorry," he sobbed. "Orbit, I'm so sorry."

In the morning, he cut the grass. In the afternoon, he got out his suitcase, and in silence packed it. In the golden light of evening, he hugged me on the oval lawn. "Leonard and Petra will take care of you until Bettine comes back," he said, and before the sun set, he drove away in the jeep.

Leonard whistled.

I know. Slowly, I followed him down to the guesthouse.

When Bettine came home, she was very sad. Leonard didn't take me to the airport like Peter did, but when Leonard left us together in the house, Bettine burst into tears, and I knew why. "It was so cruel, Orby," she said. "One day, I got this wonderful email from you, telling me how you had fooled Peter in the Orbit game. I rode the horses in Iceland...so happy...and then, a few day's later, he emails me to tell me he has gone back to her. This, Marie...what is this hold she has over him!" I just looked into my mistress' eyes. She buried her face in my fur, and we lay together on the floor. It seemed like we lay together for a long time before we finally went to bed.

The latter summer was very hot, and Leonard's tomatoes and other plants shriveled in the garden for lack of water. Then, one afternoon, Peter came back. I was a little distant this time. I sensed that Bettine felt nervous to see him, too. *My task is to take care of her. Peter has let us down.*

"I'm so dreadfully sorry," he sobbed again. "She found me in the park. I was so happy that you and I were together again, and then I looked up and there she was. A few moments later and I would have left the park and come home, but she cast some sort of spell on me. We had dinner, we talked, and somehow she persuaded me to go back. I didn't know what to say to Orbit when I came home. I felt absolutely dreadful. But it isn't working out. I miss you so much."

"Don't expect me to just take you back!" Bettine shouted.

"I don't know what to expect. We're not yet divorced. I just have nowhere to go...and I love you. I'll always love you."

They hugged each other and cried, but it was not the same. I knew it was not the same. It was more as if Peter was a guest in our house, although I felt a little of that old spark when I followed them riding out early in the morning, before the sun got too hot. I couldn't help thinking of that morning, two years ago, when they held hands together in the meadow at Finley Farms.

Not long after Peter returned, Leonard and Petra moved out of the guesthouse. Joanne and Job came to dinner, served in the old style on the screen porch. Bettine asked if they could think who might caretake for her when she and Peter were away. Apparently, she and Peter had decided to travel together on a concert cruise around the British Isles. "How about the bikers?" Joanne suggested. "Billy and Loretta say that they're looking for a new place."

"Brendan and Rhoda?"

"Yes."

And so it was that new caretakers came to Alpha Meadows. They brought furniture with them, lots of gaudy decorative stuff that Rhoda called, their "Tacky Elvis" clutter from some country store they used to run.

I went with Peter and Bettine to the airport where the security man, who knew me so well, petted me.

"Be good," Bettine said. "Take care of Peter until he comes to England."

Now, Peter and I were alone.

The next day, I watched Peter as he waded into the terrace pond to feed the water lilies. *Maybe it is like old times?* And from then on, I warmed to him again. The following day, we were sitting together on the terrace, when Peter started staring at the pond. "Is that a frog, Orbit," he said, standing up. "That has to be the biggest frog I've ever seen." The bullfrog moved among the lily pads. I started to stare at it myself, easing nearer to the pond. I thought I could see a deep shadow beneath the frog when it moved out into the open water. "Good Lord, that's no frog!" Peter yelled. "That's got to be a snapping turtle!" Peter ran for the net, and tried to scoop the turtle up. The net bent with the turtle's weight, water running off the creature's shell, and its long neck with a head of fierce teeth lashed out, while the turtle hissed. Slowly, Peter eased the animal out of the pond, and I could see its lengthy, crusted tail. I started to bark. "Back Orbit!" Peter shouted. "This thing is primitive and monstrous." I watched as Peter carried the netted turtle away, over the lawn and into the woods.

Peter seemed visibly shaken when he returned. "Can you believe it, Orby?" he said, caressing my ears. "That thing must have been in the pond when I waded in and fed the lilies yesterday. Wow....!"

I moved into the shade, panting, as peace returned.

About a week later, it was Peter's time to pack. He hugged me goodbye, and Brendan drove him to the airport. That night, I slept among the "Tacky Elvis" items in the guesthouse. I dreamed of giant armadillos and snapping turtles.

My House and Windmill right after I moved in

With Peter during the building of the House

With Bettine at Alpha Meadows

With Peter in the Spring among the Forsythia at Alpha Meadows

I love you

Alpha Meadows and my Oval Lawn and the Carport
Deck where I liked to sleep at night under the stars

On the Carport Deck at Alpha Meadows

Cavorting with Angelo in the Snow

Dominique and Angelo

Angelo kissing Harry Trotter

With Bettine at Holly's firepit

One of Peter's sketches of Woolly that hung near the
front door of Alpha Meadows. Woolly was a dog from
Peter's past with whom I felt a connection

Alpha Cat

Community Dinner on the Terrace

That was tasty…More!

Alpha Meadows from the Lawn

With Bettine in Peter's Garden at Alpha Meadows

With my Beloved Bettine at Alpha Meadows

I am about to sing

New Years Eve at Alpha Meadows

Me Magnificent?

With Bettine in the Woods

Peter with Alpha Cat

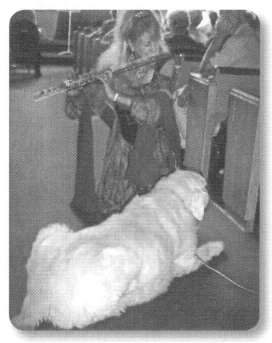

In the Unity Church, Springfield

With Bettine at CD and Book Signing, Unity Church, Springfield

With Emma, Alex, and Nanette, at Unity Church, Springfield

With Bettine and Emma, at Unity Church, Springfield

With Bettine after the Concert, Christ Episcopal Church, Springfield

Me with the Conservatory of the Ozarks people after
Bettine's Christ Church, Springfield, Concert

With Bettine on the Terrace at Alpha Meadows

Bettine, Angelo, Ninja, and Me on the Oval Lawn

In the woods with Bettine, Amadeus, and Ninja

Ninja

With George

Bettine playing a flute for Amadeus

The Guest House at Alpha Meadows

Bettine and Bacpac riding a Camel in Egypt. Bacpac Bear would tell me about Bettine's travels as he usually goes with her as a Bodyguard and Cultural Ambassador

Bettine playing flute for a Penguin on her South American Concert Tour, the last tour she took with Peter

Bettine playing with The Piano Princess. I loved the Piano Princess

Waiting for Bettine in the Explorer at the Airport

Parking Lot reunion at the Airport

Guarding my Kingdom at Alpha Meadows

Time Out with students at the Nixa Junior High School

With Bettine in the Botanical Center, Springfield Botanical Gardens

With Peter in his 'Cowboy Hat' for the Blossoms and
Blues Festival, The Springfield Botanical Gardens

Me as a Polar Bear with Peter as Kris Kringle or the White 'Santa,'
at the Botanical Center, The Springfield Botanical Gardens

With Bettine at Marie's house

My memorial Bench overlooking Peter's English
Garden in the Springfield Botanical Gardens

Bettine playing flute for Angel in Bavaria

Bettine with her neighbor Helena, and Penny and Angel, in the
Bavarian Alps, after I have gone over the Rainbow Bridge

CHAPTER ELEVEN

Caretakers

"Oh, the joy of reunion."

I GOT USED TO BRENDAN and Rhoda, but they didn't pay as much attention to me as Leonard and Petra. *I wonder where Leonard and Petra went?* Rhoda spent a lot of time on her computer, but she was good about seeing that Alpha and I had our food. Brendan worked on his bike and tinkered with the lawn mowers. He cut the grass regularly when Peter and Bettine were traveling, but he didn't grow things like Leonard, and there were lots of apples just falling from the orchard trees. Shortly after Peter and Bettine came home, however, Leonard drove up in his truck, and he and Petra picked as many apples as they could.

I was happy to see Leonard again. I lay in the orchard, while they picked away. Bettine came out.

"Won't you and Petra stay for supper?" she asked.

"Sure," Leonard said, patting my head. "By the way, I'll come back soon and start pruning. Some of these trees could do with a good pruning."

Bettine looked up at the branches. "Arlo used to prune them," she said.

I hadn't seen Arlo for a long time. I think when Brian left our community, Arlo did too, although Maryloulena and the boy were still living up in the woods behind the community cabin. I would sometimes see them when I was following the horses. Sometimes, I explored that new cabin that Susan had built, but no-one lived there now. In fact, it smelled strange—sort of mildewy. Clive was still in the cabin just below Susan's, and he was usually friendly. Sometimes, he still called me Chucky, though. *Well, those were the old days.*

Dick was still living up in the woods. I liked Dick. Actually, some nights when Peter and Bettine were away, I slept all night in Dick's cabin, even though it smelled musty. Brendan and Rhoda were not that particular about where I was, as long as I showed up for my food.

After Peter and Bettine came back, and the evenings were getting shorter, at sunset, I ran up to Dick's place. I had been there a long time when I heard the Explorer driving up to the community area. It was very dark. The car stopped, and I heard Bettine and Peter both calling: "Orbit!" I looked up at Dick and gave a short half-bark. Dick opened the cabin door and shouted into the darkness, "Orbit's here; he's with me." A flashlight then turned in Dick's direction. I got up, stretched my back legs and walked out of the cabin.

"Orbit! We've been looking everywhere for you," Bettine said.

Dick laughed. "Oh, he often comes up here and sleeps with me a while."

I wagged my tail and nuzzled Bettine.

"Come on home, Orby," she said.

I jumped up into the back seat of the Explorer. *Another Orbit game win!*

Summer turned to fall, and Bettine went traveling yet again. Peter was often away in the daytime, but he surprised me one day when he came back in the evening with two big suitcases. He was very pleased to see me sitting in my usual place on the oval lawn. "Good doggie," he said. "You're guarding the house." I slept with Peter that night. He held me in his arms. I knew he wanted to tell me something. "I'm afraid," he said. "I wish we could all go somewhere else…somewhere where we could make a new start. Alpha Meadows is killing us." He was staring up at the ceiling, but then he looked me in my eyes. "We checked out places in England and Ireland, Orby. I thought, maybe I could get work in England, but everything there is so expensive." He squeezed me. "Orby, they would put you in quarantine, that would be so hard." *Quarantine? What's that?* "It wouldn't be fair on you, Orby. Maybe, we should go back to Sea Island." *Where's that?* "Maybe, I can work at the Cloister." I could see he was sad, but I also felt his fear. *This is more than Alpha Meadows.*

It must have been that Thanksgiving time again, because two days later, we drove down to Finley Farms. Joanne's mother and father were there, and they seemed particularly happy to see Peter. Those wonderful meaty smells were drifting from the kitchen, and later, everyone sat around that big table. Joy was there. It was nice to see Joy. *I still wish Joy worked in our garden. She always talked to me, and often brought Bear with her. But Bear...I haven't seen Bear since Michael walked out of their cabin that day. What happened to Bear?* Peter fed me a chunk of turkey. I licked my paws and crossed them. I could see everyones' legs under the table. Then, they all raised their glasses and said, "To Bettine, on her travels." *I wonder where Bettine is? All she said at the airport was that she would be away a long time.*

Peter then patted me on the head. With my tongue hanging out, I looked up into his eyes. "I'm going to see Bettine in a couple of weeks. We're going to visit the penguins in South America," he said.

Joanne's mother looked so pleased. "That's wonderful!"

I thought about penguins. *I think that's what they called those funny stuffed animals that Alpha wrecked. Alpha didn't like those penguins! They looked like birds, but rather upright birds with big beaks. Alpha pulled the stuffing out of them.*

The very next day, Peter said, "I have to go away again." He seemed a little nervous. "I'll be back in a few days. I'm going to Georgia." *Peter and Bettine quite often talk about Georgia—Sea Island...the Cloister...St. Simons Island. Oh well, I suppose I'll just have to go back to "Tacky Elvis" at the guesthouse.*

I settled into spending my nights in the guesthouse among the clutter. I never did find out what "Tacky Elvis" means, but it was something I just picked up from Joanne, and it was how Peter described the guesthouse while Rhoda was there. My interpretation of "Tacky Elvis" was simply that, unlike up at Alpha Meadows, everything in the guesthouse seemed very crowded—too much stuff.

The guesthouse was decorated with all sorts of greenery, banners, and strange blown-up beings that glowed. "Christmas, Orbit," Rhoda said. "We just love Christmas." There was a warm intimacy from the lights entwined in the greenery that twinkled around the fireplace and windows, but there was almost nowhere to stretch out. Alpha had the best place—the sofa. *When she moves from there, I'm going to take her place.*

It was only a few days, and Peter came back. "Sea Island's not the same," was all he said. He then put a huge tree up in the great-room. He festooned it with lights and colored balls. I remembered these trees in the past, when all the community people would come to our house for a feast, but that didn't happen any more. Like Rhoda, they used to call it, Christmas. *Maybe, we're going to have Christmas again?* Peter spent a whole evening wrapping up parcels, while I lay on the rug in front of the big fireplace. The parcels piled up around the tree. Peter looked happy, and when he had finished, he lay down beside me on the rug in front of the fireplace. Flaming logs hissed and crackled. "When Bettine and I come back from South America, we're going to have Christmas, Orby. You, too. There are parcels for you—lots of parcels. I can see a parcel for you from Alpha, and even one from Harry Trotter." I sighed and rubbed my head on the rug as I moved my front feet in quick little motions. "Happy Orbit!" Peter said, before he snuggled into the fur of my back. We both lay contentedly in front of the fire, and the lights twinkled from the big tree. *Bliss.*

The next day, however, Brendan and Rhoda drove Peter to the airport and I was left to guard the house.

The weather changed. It rained a lot, and I sheltered under the Explorer. Then it started to snow. I had never bothered with my doghouse, the kennel I selected with Peter and Bettine at the animal store. It still stood on that platform Clive had built right beside the mud room deck. As the snow came down, I ventured inside. It was dry and a good vantage point. Through the haze of drifting flakes, I could see the horses and Dominque in their paddock. It was very quiet in the snow, and I fell asleep.

Rhoda came looking for me at dusk. She peered in. "Orbit. I've never seen you in your kennel. Could you really fit through this door?" *Of course.* I emerged from within, but it was a tight fit. *Time for my food?* And back we went to the "Tacky Elvis" and those inflatable snow people.

The snow didn't stay around for long, but it was about this time that Ninja came into my life. I ventured up to Laughing Dragons Lodge and met this black Labrador sitting on the gravel circle in front of the house. She stood up, and at first, just barked at me, but when I got closer to her, her tail wagged, and she came up and we started to sniff each other.

It wasn't long before Kiri opened the front door. "Off Orbit!" she shouted. "Ninja! Come here."

Ninja cast her eyes at me, before slowly walking toward Kiri, her tail drooping. I watched as they went into the house.

Kiri looked back at me one more time. "Off Orbit!" she repeated, before closing the door. *Why doesn't she like me? I've always tried to be nice to her, and Fred and I get along just fine.* I felt smug as I thought of Fred. *I wonder what she would think if she knew Fred sometimes lets me watch the moving pictures with him?*

I turned and wandered back to our orchard, past the shed with the mowers, and settled down to guard my house again, just like Ninja outside Laughing Dragons Lodge. I already knew, however, that Ninja and I would be friends. Just through our senses, we could tell we liked each other. She smelled right.

I went with Rhoda to the airport when Peter and Bettine came back. I sensed there was something not right, although they both made a great fuss over me when they got to the Explorer, but they seemed too quiet in themselves—awkward.

"It was a long flight, Orby," Bettine said, holding my paw on the back seat. "We came all the way from Chile."

"We had snow," Rhoda said. "Maybe, it'll snow again for Christmas?"

"We're only home two days," Bettine answered. "We have to go to England for Christmas."

Two days...they're always away. I looked up at Bettine with pleading eyes.

But, that night, when the lights went on at Alpha Meadows, everything seemed to be all right. I had almost forgotten about the big tree Peter had put up in the great-room with all those parcels in their colored papers. Now, it twinkled with lights, and Peter lit the logs in the fireplace. He kissed Bettine. "Happy Christmas! Whatever will be, let's make this a wonderful Christmas. Just you, and me, and Orbit, before we go to England and break the news."

What news?

I settled down in front of the crackling fire, as Peter and Bettine drank from crystal glasses. When we all went upstairs, I jumped up on the bed. *No "Tacky Elvis" tonight.* I lay and sighed between them. Alpha jumped up and joined us. Alpha usually stayed at Alpha Meadows. She only rarely came down to the guesthouse.

We woke to one of those really bright winter mornings, and Bettine suggested that we should take the horses out. I waited on the oval lawn, while she and Peter got Amadeus and Angelo ready. Once they were in the saddle, I followed them as I always did—down past Trail's place and all the way to the riverbed where we crossed into the area that used to be the vegetable gardens. *It's all weeds and grass now, but I can remember the past cries of the community members working in these gardens when they all called me, Fluff.* I felt sad, and stopped to sniff the rotting grass stems in the morning frost. *Where are they all now?*

When I looked up, the horses were near the pavilion. I ran to catch up. Through the meadow beside the swimming hole we went. *This was Bear's territory, but he's gone, too.* We raced up the hill, past that interesting pile of timber that they said was "Joanna's barn." *They never put it together.* There was Clive's cabin, and that empty one that Susan had built. I followed the horses, running through the bare woods beside the trail until it ended at that gate into our neighbor's field where cows grazed.

The horses were steaming. Peter kept saying "Good boy, Amadeus. You've been such a great horse," and he patted Amadeus' neck. They turned round after a short rest and started back down the trail, down the hill to the other cabins. Dick came out and waved at us, and further on, there was Clive, with a spanner in his hand, grinning like he always did, standing beside the bare chassis of a vehicle. Smoke rose from the chimney of the community cabin, and I thought I could smell the waft of a late breakfast. *Maybe, there are sausages there for me?* I remembered how Brian used to pass sausages to Rajah and me, and how Maryloulena used to scold him. "Don't waste good sausages on Chucky," she would say. *Well, I guess Dick and Clive have cooked breakfast this morning.* Angelo snorted, and way in the distance, I thought I could hear the cries of Dominique. He never liked being left behind when Peter and Bettine took out the horses. Slowly, we all went down the steep hill back to the riverbed. Then it was time for that final run up to Trail's place. Trail barked as we went past, and I stopped and barked back. *Those were great days when we roamed together, but now he was never free.*

Soon, we were back at Harry Potter's pen, and the horses were tied to the fence while Peter and Bettine removed the saddles. Harry made little snorting noises. Dominique rubbed his head on the rails. They were both always so happy when we came back. Panting, I lay down on the oval lawn. It was nice to have been out with the horses again. *Peter and Bettine are hardly ever here these days.*

I dozed in the sunlight until the lawn fell in shadow. There was that orange light before the sun disappeared—the sign of the end of a fine winter's day. It played on the post and rails of the horses' field. Why, it was time for the Orbit game, but Peter came out and brought me inside. "No Orbit game tonight," he said, entering the kitchen. "Tonight is a special night."

Wafts of cooking came from the stove. In the dining area, I could see the table was set with the crystal and polished silver. Our food was already in our bowls, but Alpha wasn't there, so I ate hers.

Peter and Bettine disappeared. I settled down in front of the fire in the great-room. When they came back, they were both dressed in fancy clothes, and they sat by the hearth and drank from small glasses. "Happy Christmas, Orbit," Bettine said, motioning her glass toward me. *Oh, Christmas.* I remembered that the humans always seemed to make a big thing of this Christmas, just like that Thanksgiving.

Eventually, we went to the dining room. The kitchen was still full of those wonderful smells, and there was chicken for me. Alpha jumped up into Bettine's lap. She got little pieces of chicken, too. There was more raising of crystal glasses. Peter and Bettine sat at the table a long time, talking a lot, but not laughing much, except with us—Alpha and me.

Afterward, we all sat near the fireplace, and one by one, Peter kept giving us parcels from under the big tree. *Summer sausage?* I could smell it through the paper. I nuzzled it. There were little cans for Alpha; a bone and big cans for me. Clothes, books, candles, piled up beside Bettine and at the foot of Peter's chair. There were parcels from the horses, parcels for the horses, and some things for Harry Trotter. *Christmas.* But, by now, I had my teeth in the bone. It wouldn't crack. It tasted good, but it was a strange kind of bone. I could crunch those deer bones in the woods, but not this one. It was sort of leathery.

"So many things from Angelo and Amadeus," Bettine said. "They must have spent all their money."

Peter smiled. "They like the dollar store."

Bettine picked up Alpha. "And you, Alpha, you went shopping, too." Then she petted me, "And you, Orbit? You all got us so many things." Alpha purred, but I had the bone more on my mind at that moment. I held it with my paw and crunched at it with my teeth.

There was colored wrapping-paper all over the floor, but eventually we went upstairs. The fire flickered on the walls of the great-room, and a clear moon shone from a winter's night through the big windows.

The next day, the suitcases were out. We drove to the airport with Rhoda. After Peter and Bettine said "Goodbye," we left—just Rhoda and me.

To my surprise, back at the guesthouse, Rhoda and Brendan started talking about Christmas, and a large inflatable man in a red suit stood among the "Tacky Elvis" stuff and the snow people. *Maybe, Christmas is yet to come? Maybe, there will be more summer sausage and bones?*

A couple of days after Bettine and Peter went away, strangers came to the guesthouse—two grown-ups and three children. The children spent a lot of time hugging me and tapping me on my head. I let them. *But, who are they?* They called Brendan "Uncle B" and Rhoda, "Auntie." *They must be part of their family.*

Rhoda was busy in the kitchen. Lots of good smells, more packages and more wrapping paper—*it must be Christmas all over again? So where's my summer sausage?* I found my space near that large, inflatable, white-bearded man in the red suit, and flopped down.

Later in the day, they let me out to do my business, and guess what—I saw Ninja in the woods. I barked and we ran toward each other. Her tail wagged, and I knew I liked my new friend. We wandered back up the hill and went down to explore around M and M's place. It didn't look as if there was anyone there, so we turned back to the horse field. Amadeus and Angelo were pulling on pieces of old hay, but I thought I should run after Dominique, just to show Ninja that I was in charge. The donkey kicked and brayed. Ninja wasn't impressed. She started to wander back toward Laughing Dragons Lodge. I caught up with her, but I instinctively knew that when we came to Kiri and Fred's land, I would not be welcome, so we playfully roughed each other up in the open meadow beyond our fields, before Ninja ran home. I barked after her and turned back down the hill into the woods close by the guesthouse, where I sniffed in the leaves to see if I could find a smelly deer bone. *That's probably what Ninja was doing down here, anyway.*

Brendan came out and whistled. I barked and ran in his direction. "Want to go up with me and do the hay?" he asked. And back we went up the hill to the horse paddock. Guess what, it was Dominique that pulled from the fresh pile first, but Angelo butted him away when Dominique went back for more.

Right after Christmas, it turned pretty cold. Soon, it was snowing again. When I was outside, little ice balls formed in the crevices of my paws. When I came in, I licked at them until they melted, leaving little pools on the floor. When Alpha went out in the snow, she looked very strange, lifting up her paws and shaking them every two or three steps, but her paws were too small to collect ice balls.

When Peter and Bettine came home, they both seemed very serious. That night, I heard the "divorce" word again.

Bettine looked at Peter. "Remember what your father said, 'I hope that in the time you are apart you will discover how much you had when you were together. You'll never know how much you'll miss.'"

Peter glanced at me and then at Bettine.

The next morning, Peter took down the big tree with all the lights and packed it up in a box. In silence, he filled two suitcases with clothes.

I went down and lay by the front door. *He's going away again. And he's taking a lot of clothes with him. I'm not going to let him out of the door.*

Bettine spent most of the day alone in her study, but when Peter brought the suitcases down, she came out, and they hugged each other and kissed.

"Take care of Orbit," Peter said. "I love Orbit so much."

I didn't move to let Peter open the front door. He knelt down and hugged me, too. They were obviously both trying to hold back tears, but I knew they were crying. "I'm so sorry, Orbit," Peter said, and picking up one suitcase, he forced the door open, making me move. Bettine held me.

When both suitcases were in the blue jeep, Peter drove away, the headlights of his car catching the white landscape, while Bettine and I watched. We stood there until the jeep rounded the corner at Laughing Dragons Lodge. Then Bettine burst into tears and pulled me back into the house.

I next saw Peter when he was sick, and Bettine brought him some chicken soup. We drove up to the back of this group of low buildings, and went into a small room where Peter was in bed. It was still icy outside, but I didn't like this room. It smelled awful, worse than Dick's cabin.

We saw him again, about two weeks later. It was in a different place. A bigger room that smelled much better. It was close to the place where Bettine took her flutes to be mended. Peter came with us, and we went to the rice restaurant. After they came back to the Explorer, Bettine put down the box of rice and other tasty tidbits for me. I climbed out of the car and wolfed them down. We took Peter back to that room, but we didn't stay. Bettine just hugged him, and then we drove away. *Divorce. I don't like divorce.*

It wasn't long before Bettine was off again, and I was back with the "Tacky Elvis" people. There was a little bit more room now, because the snow people and the big, blown-up man in the red clothing had been put away somewhere. Actually, it was cozy there with Brendan and Rhoda. Just as at our house, there was a nice warm fire of burning logs. I often lay in front of it, toasting myself on those winter days.

On one, crisp, clear day, I followed Brendan and Rhoda to the fire pit, where they burned bags of trash. They lit the fire and tended it for a while. The sun was shining, but a breeze ruffled my coat as I sat watching the flames flickering and the smoke rising up and blowing toward Laughing Dragons Lodge. The burning trash smelled pungent. When the fire died down, Rhoda and Brendan went back to the guesthouse, but I stayed where I was and rolled over on my back, rubbing it against the dry, winter grass. That felt good. A stronger gust of wind blew over Alpha Meadows. Sparkling, red embers rose in the smoke from the fire pit, then swirled to the ground. It was only a moment, but suddenly I saw little flames coming from a spot in the grass. White smoke rose, and the little line of flickering flames grew. I put my head down and stared at them. *Fascinating.* But as the area of flames increased, showing blackened grass, I sensed that this was not good. I started to bark at the burning grass. I remembered seeing this before, and how Peter was so afraid. *No, this is not good.* I barked fiercely, hoping Rhoda or Brendan would hear me. Instinctively, I bounded down the hill, closer to the guesthouse.

Rhoda opened the sliding-glass door and came out on the deck. "What is it, Orbit?"

I continued to bark. I even howled.

Rhoda and Brendan were soon up the hill again, and we ran toward the fire. There was a thick wall of smoke now, and the flames had reached the taller grass and brush between the lawn and another of our horse fields. A small cedar tree caught on fire and blazed up furiously. Yes, the flames were now much bigger, and the smoke more dense.

"The barn!" Rhoda yelled.

Brendan ran to the wooden shed where Peter kept his lawn mowers and many other things. He came out with a shovel, and started to beat at the flames, but the wind was blowing the fire right at him, and he was forced to retreat back to where Rhoda and I watched. The flames danced around the windmill and on toward the shed. "Call 9-1-1," Brendan yelled. "This is getting out of control." Rhoda ran back down to the guesthouse.

The orchard fence started to burn, and the fire edged toward the apple trees. Brendan ran in with the shovel, and again, started to beat out the flames. By the time Rhoda came back, larger flames rose up in the smoke. "It's reached the shed!" Brendan yelled.

"They're on their way!"

The wooden building started to blister and crack, and flames lept out of the window opening. The smoke turned black, and there were loud explosions from within. A half-dead tree beside the shed caught on fire, and then I heard Ninja barking from the other side.

By the time those fire trucks came, the shed was gone—nothing but a pile of debris and the grotesque black outlines of destroyed machinery, but the tree was burning furiously. *It reminds me of the flames that shot up the hollow trunks of those dead trees in the woods right after Peter and Bettine built Alpha Meadows.* The firemen shot water on the hissing remains of the shed and its contents, and soaked the ground in the path of the flames. The flames shrunk and died, and the smoke became thinner and more translucent.

I looked up at Rhoda. I think she was crying. "Oh, Orbit. What will Peter and Bettine say?" she sobbed.

Meanwhile, Brendan had stamped out the fire in the orchard. Ninja came over to us, her tail wagging. She didn't seem afraid. I remembered Trail and that other fire. *We dogs are not afraid.* But just as I had felt Peter's fear then, I sensed Rhoda's fear now.

I became quite bold with Ninja. We would often explore the woods together close to Laughing Dragons Lodge. We heard a car turn in to the drive. I knew the sound; it was Peter's jeep. I ran out of the woods and chased the jeep up the drive. The vehicle slowed down and stopped. Peter opened the door and ruffled my head. "So what's all this about a fire?" he said, as he surveyed the orchard and the blackened area where the garden shed had stood. I could still smell the charred timber and twitched my nose. "It looks like that tree burned," Peter noted. "And it even came into the orchard, but the windmill seems okay. You want to hop in, Orbit?" I rode with Peter up to the house.

In a short while, another car drove up. I didn't recognize the sound. I barked and growled as it approached. The driver was wary of me when he pulled up, but when Peter came out to meet him, I stopped barking. They both went into the house, and I settled down on the oval lawn. Ninja joined me.

After a while, Peter and the stranger, a thin-looking man in smart clothes, walked out to the burned area. We followed. Peter seemed distraught. "Everything was in there," he said. "My seven-thousand-dollar lawn mower, a push mower, my large tiller, chain saw, many suitcases… all our garden tools. The shed itself was worth about three-thousand dollars. It was custom built." The man was writing things down. Then they inspected the windmill.

Returning to his car, the stranger handed Peter a lot of papers before he drove away. I nuzzled up to Peter. *It's all something to do with the fire. Peter's upset. He needs me.*

Soon after, Rhoda and Brendan drove up in their truck. Peter and I went to the guesthouse. "The firepit had died right down," Rhoda explained. "We came back here, and then Orbit alerted us that something was wrong. By the time we got out again, the tall grass was on fire."

"I tried to stop it reaching the shed, but it was too much for me. The heat was blowing right in my face," Brendan added.

"It's nobody's fault," Peter said. "The main thing is nobody was hurt, and Orbit was okay."

I nuzzled up to all three of them.

"The insurance man was here today," Peter continued. "He wants to know everything that was lost."

"All our Christmas things were in there," Rhoda said, "the trees, the lights…the inflatables."

"My tools," Brendan added. "My tools alone are a thousand-dollar loss."

Peter started to write things down. "They want a value on everything." Then, he smiled. I felt pleased, he seemed less afraid. "I see the other Country Clipper lawn mower is down here. I wondered about that. I could only see the burned out frame of the one at the shed."

"Yes, it was down here all winter."

I saw a deer cross the road below the guesthouse, and I barked, then walked back with Peter to the jeep.

Peter came by again the next day. I was glad to see him, but he only stayed long enough to go over those papers with Rhoda and Brendan. I stayed with Rhoda and Brendan until Bettine came home.

While she was home, I went with Bettine to Springfield, where we had lunch at the rice restaurant with Peter. When they came out with my portion in a little white box, Peter said, "Orbit, I miss you so much. I work in Branson now. I have to live here in Springfield, but I want you to come and see my little house."

"We can't today," Bettine answered. "I have an appointment in fifteen minutes. But, we will."

Bummer.

A few days later, after Bettine left again, a U-Haul van arrived. It was Peter driving. He had Clive with him. They packed most of the furniture in the big room downstairs into this van, along with some of the paintings in the house.

On her return, Bettine and I met Peter in Springfield at the rice place again, and then followed him out to the north of the city. We came to a tiny house in front of which Peter had planted flowers in urns. Inside, were all those familiar bookcases and the big desk. They smelled just like they had at Alpha Meadows. I went around the house inspecting everything. *So, this is where Peter lives.* We stayed the night there, and I slept on the floor beside the bed. It was a cozy place, but I really didn't understand why we couldn't all be together at our home, as in the past.

"Now that Peter works in Branson," Bettine explained when she saw my sad eyes, "he has to get up early and drive there from Springfield every morning,"

During the summer, Peter often came back to Alpha Meadows to cut the grass, but he never stayed. Brendan and Rhoda left, and Peter and Clive moved the furniture from the guesthouse into our empty room downstairs. That evening, Peter did stay for a meal with Bettine on the terrace. It seemed like old times. Happy and content that the good times might be back, I ran off to chase a tribe of armadillos. But later, Peter drove off into the darkness. I watched the headlights of his car round the corner at Laughing Dragons Lodge. *I don't think he will ever come back.*

For the next month, Bettine was my constant companion. I followed her when she rode Amadeus or Angelo. We went on trips together in the Explorer, and in the evenings we sat on the terrace, before retiring up to the loft bedroom. We would snuggle together until I let her know I wanted to go out on the deck. There, I slept under that great canopy of stars, and heard the sounds of the night and the occasional munching of those pesky armadillos.

One day, there was a flood in the back room downstairs that soaked the carpet in the guest bedroom. Mr. Pennington came out from Seymour and laid a new carpet. For a while, there was a strange smell downstairs, but I liked the new carpet. It was soft.

A couple of days before Bettine left on her travels again, new caretakers arrived. They brought two trucks of stuff and unloaded it all at the empty guesthouse. When they had finished unpacking, they left. I went down there and looked in the sliding-glass doors from the deck. *Tacky Elvis all over again.* A great wooden machine sat in the living room surrounded by stuff. I sniffed around the deck. *What's this?* I could smell dog. The next day, these people came back with more stuff, and there was the dog. At first, she was not very friendly to me, and I thought it best not to hang around the guesthouse. I returned to Alpha Meadows, only to find the depressing sight of the suitcases. *Oh! No. I don't want Bettine to go away anymore. I don't want to be left alone with these new people. And I don't know about that dog either.*

The new caretaker's name was Robert. He came with us to the airport in the Explorer. When we pulled up at the terminal building, Bettine held my paw, and then she hugged me like she always did, "I'll be gone for a month. Guard the house," she said. Robert helped carry her suitcases into the airport terminal, while I stayed in the car. When he came back, Bettine was gone. Robert drove us home to Alpha Meadows. He picked up my dog bowls, and I walked with him down to the guesthouse. *I wonder what this will be like. My new caretakers.*

I got used to Robert and his wife. Her name was Clara. Bettine called them, the Carneys. *I suppose that's their name, Robert and Clara Carney.* Clara spent a lot of time working at the big wooden machine, making blankets. There were lots of different colored balls of wool that she wove into the machine. It clicked and clacked. She called it, a loom. Every so often, she got tired, and lay down on the floor, resting her head on my body. I let her, but I'm not sure their dog liked this very much. The dog's name was Asha. She had a smooth, brown coat and rather spindly legs. Her face was striped, somewhat like a cat's. Ninja and I thought her very strange. But in time, the three of us became good friends.

Clara took me to Aunt Ellen's, and after my bath, to my horror, Aunt Ellen cut off all my coat. I looked as thin as Asha, and my skin was wrinkled. There was nothing left to dry. I remembered how Bettine and Peter had said they would never give me a buzz—that time when Gabriel suggested I should have a buzz, just like he and his father. I remembered how dreadful poor Bear looked after Michael and Joy had buzzed him. Now, I looked the same—simply dreadful. But, I didn't blame Aunt Ellen. I just knew this buzz cut was Clara's idea.

Bettine was horrified when she came home. She gasped. "What's happened to Orbit?" Clara tried to explain that it was for my benefit in the great heat. *Doesn't Clara know that we long-haired, white dogs actually feel cooler in the heat than shorter-coated, black and brown dogs?*

My now thin tail was hanging between the virtually visible bones of my legs, and the size of my paws was ridiculously exaggerated. "Your ears look like those of a mountain goat," Bettine said. I just didn't look like a Great Pyrenees, and I felt ashamed. My pride was hurt, and it was a while before I dared show myself to Ninja. But, in time, my coat did start to grow back.

When Bettine was home, we shared wonderful times together, but during this period she was away more than she was home. Sometimes, when she was at Alpha Meadows, a man called George visited, who always took lots of photographs of me, but not until I was a semblance of my old self again—unbuzzed! *Fortunately, my coat grows fast.* I had learned about photographs, at least in as much as I knew what people who carried these cameras expected of me. Peter had always taken lots of photographs of me, mostly with Bettine, and sometimes, when I was singing to the sound of her flutes. I actually liked it. It was fun, and I often moved my front feet in satisfaction, scraping the earth or the carpet as if I was going to dig a hole. Bettine said it was my "Happy Orbit" movement. George would speak to me gently, so that I would look right into his camera. I would hear it click, and I knew that made a photograph. I knew George wanted me to be still and look at him. But when the clicking finished, I still always made my "Happy Orbit" movement. George was very patient with me. He never scolded me if I looked the wrong way, and I soon came to enjoy our partnership. When he visited, I lay around on the terrace or inside by the fireplace, waiting for him to get out his camera. Sometimes, he wanted Bettine and me together, and Bettine would place her face against my head, or play flutes for me. I liked that.

One time, later that year, Bettine took me to Springfield where she was to play a concert. I hadn't seen Peter since that night we stayed with him. It seemed a long time ago now, but he was at that concert. Marie was with him. She was that girl from the writers' conference. I knew it was she. She smelled just the same. I sat with them at the back of the concert place. Marie gently held me most of the evening. Peter seemed happy, too, although a little nervous. *Does she live with him now?* While I was thinking about this, Bettine called my name. *I suppose this is like the Unity church or that theater we went to? Bettine wants me to go up to her while she is playing.* I looked up at Marie. *She wants me to sing.* Marie unclipped my leash from my collar, and I walked between the rows of chairs about half-way toward Bettine. Bettine stooped forward, playing the small flute that made the high-piercing sounds. She was looking directly at me. Notes rose in my throat, and I started to match the tune in a prolonged howl. Everyone was looking at me. But, suddenly, I felt embarrassed, and before Bettine had finished, I ran back to Marie and Peter. "Good doggie," Peter said. "You can still sing." And even though I hadn't finished my performance, many people came up to me and petted me after that concert.

Most of the time that year, however, I was on my own. I suppose that is why Ninja, Asha, and I, became such friends.

Kiri was away a lot, and Fred used to invite all three of us into Laughing Dragons Lodge where we watched his moving pictures, the ones M and M and Fred called, TV. I used to like to listen to the music. Music always made me think of Bettine. We didn't go to M and M's much anymore. They had a child now, and kept themselves to themselves, a lot more than in the past, although I always knew when their noisy truck drove up. Most the time, the three of us dogs roamed freely through the woods, digging holes, chasing rabbits, pulling on smelly deer bones or the carcass of the occasional armadillo. The woods were exciting, and we spent a lot more time in our woods than I used to. Sometimes, we crossed the road below the guesthouse and roamed farther afield.

We thought we saw a deer standing among the trees. Ninja started to run toward the beast. Asha was close behind, and I in the rear. There was a loud bang, and the deer lept up and ran off. Ninja and Asha chased after it. A voice yelled at us. There was another loud crack. Ninja fell, and before I could reach them, a third terrifying sound rang through the air, accompanied by a sinister whistle. Asha jumped and ran back toward me before stumbling in the underbrush. I could still hear shouting, and I saw two men reach Ninja. They kicked her, but she didn't get up or even bark. I crouched down beside Asha and saw blood on her shoulder. Asha was whimpering. The men moved on in the other direction.

I went back to Ninja and nuzzled her. There was lots of blood, and there was no response. Her tongue hung out, and her eyes were wide open and still. She seemed as lifeless as a dead armadillo. *Is* she *dead?* I remembered encounters with possums, which had tried to fool me this way. I gave a little whine and looked toward where Asha lay. Slowly, I walked back to her. She was very still, too, almost stiff, but she continued to whimper, and her eyes were fearful, looking right into mine. I gently placed my big paw on her back, and licked at the blood on her shoulder. She whimpered louder. *I must get Robert and Clara.* I ran back toward the road and our guesthouse half-way up our hill.

Robert was splitting wood. I stood in front of him, barking furiously. "What is it?" he said, lowering the axe. I continued to bark. He stood and looked across the valley. "Those shots," he said. "Come, Orbit, show me!"

I led Robert down the hill, across the road, and back into the woods. I knew I could find Asha and Ninja. I could smell our scent on the fallen leaves from the autumnal trees.

Asha was still whimpering and even gave a faint bark when she saw her master. Robert knelt down and stroked her. She yelped, but looked up at him. "There, there…" he said. "We're goin' to get you home. Everything's goin' to be all right."

Robert looked different as he cradled Asha. Softer, he reminded me of Johnny all those years ago. *What about Ninja?* I patted Robert's shoulder with my paw, and barked. Robert looked around. I started to walk away toward Ninja. "Ninja, too?" he said, and he stood back up and followed me.

Ninja's lifeless body was only a few trees away. "They got her, Orbit," Robert said slowly. "They might have got Asha, too. She's really hurting."

We went back and found Clara. They brought a blanket for Asha, and together they carried her home. Then we went back with a blanket for Ninja, and took her to Fred at Laughing Dragons' Lodge.

Tears ran down Fred's face.

At the guesthouse, Clara cleaned Asha's wound. Asha yelped when Clara dabbed at it with a wet cloth.

"We must get her to the vet right away," Robert said.

Robert lifted Asha into the back seat of his car. I watched. "All right, Orbit, jump in," Clara said, "but they might not let you come with us into the animal hospital." I snuggled up beside Asha on the back seat and looked into her eyes.

On the way, we had to drive through the river above the waterfall they called, Finley Falls. I had been driven across there so many times, but when we met the uneven surface and the car bounced through the shallow water above the shelf-rock, Asha yelped. I could feel her pain, and I reached for her with my paw. It wasn't long before we arrived at the animal hospital.

Robert had to carry Asha, and I followed with Clara, lifting my leg to pee on a bush along the way. The vet people let me in. I could smell that veterinary smell as we sat waiting our turn—sickly sweet. There was another small dog waiting. We sniffed each other, but I knew my task was to stay with Asha. I rested my head on Robert's knee beside Asha. My friend Dr. Espey came out. He took us into a small room and lay Asha on a table. As the vet examined her, she gave more little yelps. I responded in kind just to let her know I was still there.

"She's lucky to be alive," the vet said. "It just missed the back of her neck and deflected off the shoulder blade. She'll recover as long as we can keep the wound really clean."

They kept Asha at the animal hospital, and I felt very sad having to leave her. The next day, when we returned to see how she was doing, she was in a stall, a little larger, but like those stalls at Aunt Ellen's place where

I occasionally got taken for those baths and coat trims. I immediately went to the stall, and they let me in with Asha. She had a large cone around her head. "She's going to have to keep this on for a while to stop her from licking at the wound," Dr. Espey said. "I'll let you take her home. I'm going to give you something to dress the wound, but I want you to come back here tomorrow. It's vital we get no infection in there." I snuggled up beside Asha. Our eyes met. She licked at my fur, and I licked her front paw. Dr. Espey patted me on the head. "Good dog, Orbit," he said, "I know you're helping." I panted, but kept my eyes firmly on Asha. They carried Asha to the truck. I followed, and sat with her on the back seat.

Most that afternoon, I stayed in the guesthouse with Asha. She couldn't walk and still whimpered a lot, but she knew I was right there beside her. She struggled to get up a couple of times, but the pain in her shoulder made her howl, and she lay right back down again, her head surrounded by that cone. *That must be uncomfortable.*

Several more times, we went back to the animal hospital. Dr. Espey always told me I was a good dog. I felt the love that connected me to Asha, as she gradually recovered her strength.

As Asha got stronger, I couldn't help remembering Ninja. When we took Ninja's lifeless body to Fred at Laughing Dragons Lodge, he had cried. I knew he was sad, but as I looked up at him, a smile had come across his face. "Ninja's gone over the rainbow," he said, "to a better place." *Over the rainbow. The bridge in the sky that leads to that place where everything is forever now.*

Somehow, after Ninja died, I became very conscious of those rainbows in the sky. I saw the colors in the high-pitched notes of strange music that rang in my ears whenever that magical arc stilled the rain, and shafts of sunlight filtered through the clouds. The music made me stop, look up, and see the rainbow bridge. Then I remembered Ninja. *We are forever connected. Nothing begins…nothing ends.*

Bettine was very sad when she came home and heard about the shootings in the woods. Often, she invited Fred to come and eat with her on the terrace, knowing he had lost the companionship of Ninja. We would all share chicken and steak cooked on the barbecue. Weeds grew between the stones of the terrace now, but there was still a magical feeling as the sun set, and the moon rose, reflecting its pale face in the waters of our pond. The waterfall and the wall-fountain accompanied the sounds of the frogs and the crickets. Alpha Meadows was still a beautiful place.

On several occasions, Bettine took me with her to Unity Church. I used to like visiting Sue Baggett in her office with its big desk, and she let me stay at the back of the church during the services when Bettine had to be up front to play her flutes. I made friends with a pretty girl...Nadia. I used to sit with her and her young brother, Alex, and their friend, Emma. Nadia petted me the whole time, even when the singing bowl reverberated in the silence. Their mother was Nanette, the lady who had bought one of Peter's books after that talk he had given about Mary Magdalene.

Sometimes, when we went into Springfield, Bettine used to take me to this printing place where she had her music recordings and films made. I think the place was named Cantrell and Barnes. The people were very nice there and all seemed to have the name, Dave. They would let me roam around, while they discussed things with Bettine. I used to explore all their machines and packing stations in the back. Some of the workers tried to explain to me what was going on. I looked back up at them with intelligent eyes. They started to call me, the Supervisor. Bettine once explained to me that this was the place that made the films of me singing to her flutes—films that she was apparently showing all over the world at her concerts. *Many, many people I have never seen have heard me sing. Amazing!*

Then, one early evening, after Bettine had gone on her travels again, a black car drove up our drive that I had not seen before. I barked ferociously as it approached. Suddenly, I heard this voice call to me from the car window, "Orbit!" It was Peter. *Where is the jeep?* As the car slowed down to stop by the oval lawn, I sauntered over to it. Peter opened the door and petted my head. "Orbit," he choked. He was dressed in a smart suit and didn't stay long, but he cut the oval lawn. Robert hardly ever cut the grass.

A week later, he was back again and stayed all day, cutting the grass with the big, red mower that had survived the fire. He came every week and cut the grass. He also started to water the flowers. He even sprayed the weeds on the terrace with that smelly stuff he always used. Soon, they withered and died. He always shared time with me, too. I was happy to see him, but he never stayed the night.

Robert and Clara didn't pay much attention to Peter when he was here, but I liked it when he kept coming to cut the grass. I would roll on the freshly cut lawn to show my appreciation. It was as if life was slowly breathing back into Alpha Meadows. I think the horses and Dominique, looked forward to Peter's visits, too, even Harry Trotter, the pig.

Not long after this, Harry Trotter was taken away in a farmer's truck. I never saw him again. Bettine later said he had died at the farmer's place, shortly after he had become the father of six piglets.

When Bettine was home, she usually cooked a late breakfast for Peter before he started mowing. I was then allowed to lick the egg off his plate. "I missed the sound of you mowing," she said to Peter. "I never thought I would, but it's comforting to hear you mowing again." And so it went on until the grass stopped growing. Peter made his weekly visits.

The next year, Peter continued to mow, plant flowers in the terrace pots, and keep them watered. Then, one day, after he had been watering, I heard him scream in the Den. "No! Oh, no!" he shouted. "No!" I rushed to the lower level of the house. Water was pouring down the stonework by the stove and spreading across the room.

Peter ran to the safe place where we all gathered by the furnace and pumps when there was a bad storm. I don't know what he did in there, but the water stopped flowing, although by now the carpet squelched under our feet.

Over the next few days, the carpet was all removed, and big fans whirred to dry out the flooring. That insurance man came back again with his papers. *This is bad!*

Eventually, Mr. Pennington arrived with big rolls of new carpet. It was thinner than the old carpet, and it wasn't white, but speckled brown. It didn't feel as nice to lie on, but the room was restored to normality.

That summer, Robert and Clara started to paint the outside of the house, and a man built a new set of steps and a porch by the front door. The dining room was tiled like the kitchen, and from time to time strangers came to look over the house. *Something's going on?* I didn't like this invasion of my world. Men came in a big truck and they took the Steinway. Peter and Bettine were both there, and I knew they were tearful. For a moment, I heard the music of the piano princess resound in the empty space above the indentures in the carpet, marking the place where the instrument had stood. A lady called Jo Moon came to the house, and she and Bettine packed up many things in boxes and tubs. I watched in dismay as piece by piece my kingdom was dismantled.

Then one glorious evening, Peter came to the house. He had cut the grass the day before. The terrace tubs were overflowing with plants. Peter cooked a beautiful dinner. Bettine and Peter drank from those small, crystal glasses and walked out on the terrace. That music was playing... the French lady was singing. They danced, and they looked back at our home all lit up as the moon rose over the stables. "This was our creation," Peter said.

"Your creation...the most beautiful house I ever lived in," Bettine said as they held hands in the mingling glow of the illuminated façade and the growing moonlight. "If only it could have all worked out." Bettine called to me. "It gave us Orbit, our son. Orbit, you're the best thing that ever happened to us." I felt the tension and the love. I sensed the finality. Then we all danced to the music. I stood up on my hind legs, Bettine and Peter holding my paws as we swayed together. The frogs bellowed their chorus.

Peter left quite late that night, but the suitcases were out, and I sensed something more than just another journey. The big walk-in closet was almost empty. I didn't sleep much, but lay on the bed with Bettine. Peter was back in the morning, and the three of us went to the airport.

Bettine cried when she hugged me goodbye. "You've been such a good dog," she repeated, over and over again.

Then it was time to move on. Peter drove to the parking lot. He went back to the airport terminal and was there longer than usual. When he returned, he was crying.

"It's you and me, now, Orbit," he choked. "Bettine's gone to live in Bavaria."

Peter stayed with me at the house a few nights after we got back. Jo Moon finished sealing all the boxes and containers piled up in the garage guestroom. After she left, there was a terrible storm. We went down to the guestroom to sleep near the safe room. Alpha wasn't with us. She spent most of her time now with Robert and Clara. The storm raged. I could hear the rain splashing outside the sliding-glass doors. I snuggled up to Peter on the large bed. After the storm had passed, Peter got up. I heard the splash of his feet as he got off the bed. "Oh No!" he shouted. "No! Not again!" I followed him off the bed. The carpet was soaking wet. Water had poured in from under the sliding door. I lapped at it. Yes, it was water.

Jo Moon and Peter went through the boxes the next morning. They said most of them had remained dry, being in large plastic containers. The fans whirred again, and slowly the carpet dried out, although there was a strange smell that I didn't like—a mildewy smell.

"You need to get guttering up there," Jo Moon said. "That's what caused this."

Peter looked up at the bare overhanging eve. "But it's never done this before."

"That was heavy rain, and you can see how it washed away at the gravel in front of the sliding doors, causing it to pool there."

"Another expense," Peter muttered. "It never stops. Alpha Meadows has become a bottomless pit."

The carpet was barely dry again, when a big van came, and all the containers were loaded. The house looked somewhat bare. Bettine's boxes were on their way to Bavaria. Over the next few days, Peter rearranged the furniture that was left. Men came and fixed new guttering and downpipes. The house was neat and tidy, but its soul was gone. I returned to live with Alpha and Asha down at the guesthouse.

CHAPTER TWELVE

Working with Kids

"I just let them feel my love."

A FEW DAYS AFTER BETTINE left, the lady who had been grooming Amadeus and Angelo came with a big trailer and took them away. Dominique was beside himself while Amadeus and Angelo were being loaded, but it was soon his turn, too. Peter was watching, and I stood beside him. As the truck drove away, he burst into tears. I looked up at him and pawed his trousers. Then we both watched the dust settle as we stood there in an eerie silence.

The house was shut up now. I lived in the guesthouse with Asha and Alpha. Robert and Clara tried to finish painting the outside of Alpha Meadows, but they never did complete it. Peter continued to come every week and cut the grass, but he never stayed. Sometimes, I went with Asha and the Carneys to a house they had in the country. They started to pack up some of their things and take them there in the back of their truck. It was quite a long drive. Alpha didn't come, but Asha and I hung out on the back seat of the truck's cab. Asha was free of that cone now. I sat with my head on her neck. We usually slept most of the way. Asha would wake first, because she knew the smells of the area. It was a different smell to Alpha Meadows.

After our second journey to this house, our guesthouse was almost bare. Stains were now visible on the carpet, and there were burn marks in front of the hearth. I knew something was wrong when Clara came in, looked around the house, and called Asha. I got up to go with Asha, but Clara said, "No! Orbit, you must stay here with Alpha."

I saw Robert on the deck through the sliding-glass doors. He was carrying away the wrought-iron table and chairs, even the flower pots. I barked. *Something's not right.* Robert looked at me through the glass, and then carried off the last of the pots. I heard the truck rev up, and I saw it drive away. A deathly silence came over the empty guesthouse, and Alpha started walking about the house sniffing at nothing. I stared out from behind the glass doors. All of a sudden, I saw Peter running down the hill.

The front door opened.

"Orbit! Thank God you're here! They've gone. I was so afraid they might have taken you."

Alpha mewed.

"And you, Alpha."

We followed Peter back up to Alpha Meadows. It was a warm autumn day. He let us in, and then went mowing. It was dusk when he finished.

"You'll both come home with me," he said, when he came back in.

Peter found the box that they used to put Alpha in if she had to go to visit Dr. Espey.

"You're going to have to come with me to Springfield," he told us.

I sat on the back seat of Peter's black car, and Alpha mewed fearfully from the box on the front seat until we got out onto the smooth road. Our empty bowls rattled on the floor. *This is final. We're leaving our home... my kingdom.*

I knew the road to Springfield so well, but when we got there, I became confused, because we didn't go to the Unity church or any of our usual haunts. We stopped in an unfamiliar street, in the driveway of a house with a wrought-iron porch. Peter had me on a leash. "You'll have to become a city dog now," he said as we went up the steps onto the porch.

The front door opened, and there was Marie. I knew it was her. I could smell her perfume. I looked up at her. She smiled at me and stroked my ears. "Orbit!" she said.

"He's going to have to stay with us a while," Peter explained. "The caretakers have done a bunk. They left Alpha and Orbit all alone. It was a lucky thing I went out there today."

"Alpha's here?"

"Yes…in the car. Sit with Orbit, while I get her in."

A fluffy ginger cat hissed at me, but I just flopped down on the floor and made myself at home.

Peter brought Alpha in. I could tell she was scared. It turned out that there were two ginger cats prowling around, and Alpha perched herself on the end of a sofa, quivering. The room seemed dark after all the light at Alpha Meadows.

I followed Peter through the kitchen and down a flight of stairs. This was better. I recognized the smell of Peter's books, the bookcases, and so many things that I remembered from the den at Alpha Meadows. I lay down on the soft carpet. Marie joined us. She started to groom me with a kitty brush. I let her. It felt good. I rolled over on my side and waved a paw in the air.

I got used to walking on the leash when Peter and Marie took me out in this new neighborhood. We frequently stopped and talked to strangers. Sometimes, we even went into their homes. Everyone admired me. It reminded me of those old days on the courses, when so many people came to visit us at Alpha Meadows. People thought I was such a big dog, and they always wanted to pet me. These days, Peter was apparently away in Branson all day, and at times, I felt a little awkward with those ginger cats. Alpha kept her distance from them, too. She soon found her own place downstairs, where she took up residence on the sofa. The ginger cats didn't bother her much there. They rarely came down to this basement room with all its bookshelves. Alpha always slept on that sofa at night, but I wanted to sleep beside Peter in Marie's bedroom. Sometimes, the ginger cats had to pass by me, before jumping up on the bed where they snuggled up to Marie. Until they were safely on the bed, I kept an eye open. They often hissed at me as they passed.

Just as I was getting used to my new surroundings, there came a dramatic change in my life. I thought I was going for a walk as I went out on the leash with Peter and Marie, but I found out that we were going for a car ride. I became suspicious when Peter put my food and water bowls in the car. We went for a drive on that warm autumn evening. It wasn't very far, but I had no idea where we were. Eventually, we stopped in front of an old house on a leafy street. Peter got out and went to the front door. A lady and a young girl came out. I recognized them…Nanette and that adorable girl from the Unity church…Nadia.

Peter came back. "Your new home, Orby," he said. "You're going to stay with Nanette and Nadia."

"Can I walk him?" the pretty girl asked.

"Yes."

She took my leash and walked me down the street past several other large, old houses surrounded by shrubs and trees. I looked back once, and saw Peter and Marie carrying my bowls into the house. A little boy came running down the street after Nadia. "Wait for me! I want to walk the fluffy dog," he shouted.

Nadia handed the leash to him. "Now, hold on to him. He's Orbit. You know…the big dog from church."

I was walking pretty slowly, marking the trees and shrubs. We went up one side of the street and then back down the other. When we reached the house again, Peter and Marie were talking to Nanette and an older lady. A gray, wooly dog barked when I came in.

"Pele!" Nanette said.

I went up to him. Our noses met.

"He's a standard poodle?" Peter asked.

"Yes, and there are two more. They're outside in the garden…Little Jon and Robin Hood."

I found my bowls in the kitchen and lapped at the water. *Looks like I'm going to stay here now.* Pele joined me, but when he drank from my bowl, I gave a low warning growl. He then went to his own bowl.

Peter and Marie both hugged me. I heard Peter sob. I watched with Nadia as they went back to their car and drove away.

"So, the fluffy dog is going to stay with us?" the little boy said. "Can he sleep with me?"

"If you're nice to him," Nanette answered. "Now, let's take him outside to run in the yard."

No sooner were we in the backyard, and the other two dogs came running up to me. I jumped, somewhat startled. They started to sniff at me, even my private places.

"Little Jon! That's not polite," Nanette said, and she threw a stick that made the two dogs run.

They must be standard poodles, as well. It's interesting, all of us are wooly dogs.

Little Jon and Robin Hood kept chasing the stick. Pele then came out and joined them. I barked, and then ran with them, too. I knew we would all be friends. Pele was strange, though. He would jump up in the air and turn. "Can you do backflips?" Nadia asked me. *I don't know. I think that might be difficult.*

There were miniature chickens in the yard, but I noticed the poodles didn't chase them. Something deep within me took me back to that day long ago when we made that outing to Billy's and Loretta's funny dome houses where I chased the chickens. I remembered Brian being very angry with me. I've never chased a chicken since.

It was soon dark, and we all came back into the warm kitchen where the old lady was cooking. I twitched my nose. It smelled good. Later, at the kitchen table, the little boy asked, "Can the fluffy dog have some of mine?"

The old lady said, "No! Then they will all want some. You know the rules, Alex."

No steak, I realized, but I warmed to Alex.

Nadia called me upstairs when they went to bed. The bare stairs creaked. At first, I slept in Nadia's room, but the door was open, and later I slipped out and plonked myself down with a thud outside Alex's open door.

"Is that you, Fluffy Dog?" Alex whispered.

I turned my head and looked into the room. And so it was that every night I lay at Alex's door, although it was Nadia who always took me for a walk when she came home from school. *What's school?* I was soon to find out.

I discovered that Nanette was a teacher at a school. Apparently, all children go to school, although I don't remember Gabriel going to school back in the community days. I learned that to go to school you had to have a bath...*Bummer!* I had only had baths when Peter or Bettine took me to Aunt Ellen's before she trimmed my coat.

At first, I struggled, expressing dismay when Nanette tried to get me in the tub. "Orbit...you have to have a bath if you're to come to school with me. It's just one of the rules," she insisted. I looked up at her with pleading eyes. "Really...you're going to have to have a bath twice a week." *Just to go to school? There must be something very special about school. A bath at Aunt Ellen's usually meant Bettine was coming home!*

Reluctantly, I let her help me into the tub. It was full of soapy warm water that actually felt good. "You have to be very clean if you come with me to Nixa Junior High," Nanette said, scrubbing my fur. "The children will love you and they'll pet you and hug you. Now, you have to be very nice to them or they won't let you come back." After the soapy water was drained away, Nanette rinsed me off, and then rubbed me down with a big towel, before drying me with one of those hot-air machines, just like at Aunt Ellen's. I loved the feel of the warm air fluffing my fur. Gentle brushing and combing followed.

That night, Alex laughed when he saw me. "Fluffy Dog! You see Orbit really is a fluffy dog," he said, putting his arms around my neck and smelling my coat. "He smells so good, and he's so soft."

I suppose I am a fluffy dog.

"He's going to school with me in the morning," Nanette said.

"I wish he could come to our school. We don't have doggies at our school."

Well, I suppose I'm going to find out tomorrow what's so special about school.

We got up early to go to school. Nanette drove a little white car, and I sat on the back seat, wondering what the day had in store. School turned out to be a large, single-story, redbrick building somewhere south of Springfield. "Welcome to Nixa Junior High," Nanette said as she let me out of the car on my leash. I smelled the parking lot—many interesting odors. Nanette led me to a lamp post. "Pee, Orbit," she said. *No problem, I am eager to mark this school territory if it is so special.*

She took me in through glass doors and down a passageway. I was brought into a light-filled room with many identical desks, along with a big table up front where Nanette started to unload a bag of papers. There was a rug there that I just knew was meant for me. I sat on it. Not long after that, I heard the squeals of children and the banging of doors, and soon boys and girls came into our room. Nanette held my leash, but some of the children couldn't help coming up to me.

"This is the doggie? What's his name?" a little girl asked.

"Orbit," Nanette answered, "but sit at your desks. I'll tell you about Orbit when everyone's here."

A bell rang. Nanette closed the door. She called out names, and the children answered. Then she wrote something on the wall-board behind our table. "Orbit," she said when she had finished. "Orbit's the dog I've been telling you about. He's going to come to school every Friday and maybe twice a week. He's a very loving dog, and I want you all to be especially nice to him."

She made them repeat my name.

"Orbit!" they all shouted together.

Nanette let go of my leash and encouraged me to walk freely through the room. As I sniffed at the desks, and looked up at the boys and girls, many of them reached out to touch me, patting me on my head, and Nanette kept saying, "Good dog Orbit, good dog."

So, this is school?

After that, I was allowed to lie on the rug near Nanette's table and doze until the next bell jolted me back to life. Many of the children, mostly the boys, came up to me and petted me. *Wow! I started to feel really special.*

There was one boy, however, with whom I really bonded. He was bigger than most the others and boisterous. That first day, he got into trouble for shouting too much. Then he was sent to me. He lay down on a blanket beside me, and just looked into my eyes. I gently stretched out a paw and placed it on him. We just lay together, and the boy became completely calm. This happened on other days, many times.

Other boys and girls walked me when it was their break time, and some, especially the girls, brushed me. Nanette encouraged this. Apparently, by taking me on walks and brushing me, they earned "good behavior points," whatever that means. This became a pattern every time we went to the Nixa school.

"Orbit, you're wonderful," Nanette told me as I jumped up into the back seat of her white car to go home. "You give the children so much confidence. They see your kindness. These are children, who have difficult lives and can act out, but you completely calm them down." *Difficult? Act out?*

I liked to be driven around in the back seat of this car. Sometimes, we rode with the roof down, and I sat on my haunches so everybody we passed could see me, and I would turn my head from side to side with my tongue hanging out. People waved at me, and I wanted to raise a paw and wave back, but when I tried, I lost my balance.

Most weekends, we drove out to Nanette's farm at a place called Aurora. I loved it there. There were horses like Amadeus and Angelo, and a pony even smaller than Dominique. The pony was called, Princess— apparently, a Shetland. On my third visit, Princess came up on the deck of the old farmhouse and lay down beside me. Nanette fed us carrots. Princess would only eat her carrots if I had one. The carrots turned my tongue orange. After that, Princess Pony and I spent many happy hours together on the deck. *I don't think Dominique would ever lie down beside me like this.*

There was a huge bathtub at the house in Aurora, and usually, after Nanette bathed me, she took me outside where I dried off. Nanette gently rocked herself in an old creaking chair, and Princess came up the steps and joined us. We could hear the wind blowing across the land and flapping the screen doors. It fluffed my fur, and it tinkled the tubes of a hanging wind chime.

Pele sometimes came with us to Aurora, but Little Jon and Robin Hood usually stayed with the old lady, whom Nadia and Alex referred to as, "Nana." Pele and I would run together in the fields, and he would show off doing his back flips, but Princess didn't pay much attention to Pele, although he sometimes joined us on the deck.

Pele and I were becoming very close to each other, though. At "the house on Pickwick" as they called the old lady's home, Pele shared the bowl next to mine in the kitchen, and we just bonded. He quickly showed me how to open the flap so we could go out and play in the yard at any time. I could barely squeeze through the opening. Pele and I were playing outside one day when Peter came to visit. Peter was standing at the little picket fence when Nadia called to me, "Someone to see you."

Then I heard Peter's voice, "Orbit, it's me!" I ran to the fence and put my paws up.

Peter ruffled my ears. I could see his eyes were watering. "Orby!" he said. "You look happy, Orby, I miss you so much."

Peter opened the gate, and I came out. I was very used to the leash when walking on Pickwick. Peter hooked it up, and took me up and down the street. Marie was not with him. He was alone. Before we got back, Alex came running to join us. "Let me walk Fuffy Dog," he said. Peter handed Alex my leash.

When we got back, Peter hugged me and left. I went downstairs with Alex and Nadia to the place where we watched TV. I saw Peter looking down at us through the staircase window, but the next time I looked up, he was gone. Nadia and Alex sat on this cushion-strewn sofa. I sat on the floor, guarding them. Pele joined us. *That was our task…to guard Alex and Nadia. Maybe that's why I'm the only dog the old lady allows in the bedrooms upstairs?*

There were two cats, too—Bobbie, the Maincoon, and Moulder, the Angora. They were both "fluffy cats" as Alex said, but Bobbie was huge, probably three times the size of Alpha Cat. They both had big paws with tufts rather like mine. The cats tolerated me, especially when we were all downstairs, but then they were used to big wooly dogs—my gray poodle friend Pele, and those brown, and cream, poodles, Little Jon and Robin Hood. Alex said Little Jon was "a chocolate dog." *Fluffy Dog and Chocolate Dog.*

Apparently, Nanette had been going through a rough patch before I came to the Pickwick Street house. "You're my lifesaver, Orbit," she said. "My life was falling apart…no job, divorce, and then you came along. You're as much a comfort to me as you are to my kids at school. The kids can't help it, Orbit. They have an emotional disability, and have behavior disorders, but they respond to love. That's what you give them…love, just like you give me love. I think you're making Pele a much more loving dog, too. He's learning from you. You're a wise teacher."

I sensed what she was saying, and it was just as well, because a new task fell to me at Nixa Junior High School. There was this boy named Mike. He was often disruptive. Several times they had to send him away from our classroom. I wondered where he went. The day came that Nanette took him out, and I followed them to the door. I wanted to see where she took him. I looked up at Nanette. "Come with us," she said.

We went to a room they called, the library.

"This time you can share your 'Time Out' with Orbit," Nanette said to Mike. She left us alone.

Mike started to pet me. His eyes sparkled. Away from everyone else, he became completely calm in my presence. I lay on my back and put my paws in the air. Mike laughed, and we rolled on the floor. We became still, and just lay together.

Nanette smiled when she came back. "You two look so calm and happy."

We went back to the classroom. Mike was not disruptive anymore that day, and, before we left, he even brushed me at the same time as a girl named, Penny. They were both laughing.

On the way home, Nanette stopped at Petsmart, allowing me to choose a toy...a little, stuffed doggie that squeaked. Then as always happened when we went to the pet store, the check-out girl gave me a treat. *Not a bad ending to a perfect day.*

After this, I often went with Mike to the library for "Time Out." I remembered what Nanette had said, "It's not their fault. They can't help it. All we can do is love them." Mike and I really bonded.

"You can just read the kids," Nanette said to me. "You're such a help to me, Orbit"

CHAPTER THIRTEEN

The Botanical Center and my life as a Polar Bear

"On lazy summer days, drink plenty and sit under a shady tree."

IT WAS EARLY EVENING ON a warm September day. Nanette was driving the white car with the top down. I sat regally on the back seat, wondering where we were going. She had given me a bath earlier. *Perhaps we're going to school?* But, we didn't go the right way. We turned onto a quiet street, and then I knew. We slowed down and stopped in the driveway of Marie's place. *No,* I wondered. *Nanette! Are you going to leave me here?*

Peter came out. "Orbit!" he shouted joyfully. "Orbit, you look so clean."

I hadn't seen Peter for some time, but I didn't move. I sat upright in the back of the car. I didn't want to leave Nanette, Alex, Nadia, or even the old lady. *What about my doggie friends—Little Jon, Robin Hood, and my special pal, Pele? What about Princess, the pony? I thought we were going to pick Alex up from some place, but no, here we are at Marie's house.*

Marie came out. She made herself busy, talking to Nanette. Peter came over to me and opened the car door, but I stayed where I was, bolt upright. "Come, Orbit," Peter said. "It's so wonderful to see you." He rubbed the top of my head. I looked down into his eyes, for I sat taller than him in the car.

"Where've you been?" I barked softly.

Nanette turned and came back to us. "Come on out, Orbit."

I yawned.

"He loves this car," Nanette explained. "It's *his* car. Now, Orbit, come on out!"

I didn't want to get out of *my* car, but, slowly, I stepped down onto the grass. Marie came up to me and knelt down beside me. I sat on my haunches, lay down, and stretched out my front paws.

Nanette handed Peter my leash, and she put my bowls down on the porch. "Now, you be good, Orbit," she said, before getting back into the car. I looked up at her when she was sitting in the driving seat. *Are you really leaving me here? You look sad.*

The car drove away. Peter put on my leash, and with Marie, took me for a walk. This was not so bad, there were lots of new doggie smells, new trees to mark, and at one time, there were people to meet.

"Is that a polar bear?" a child younger than Alex asked.

"He's like a polar bear," Marie agreed.

By the time we got back, it was nearly dark. I followed them up the steps, and there we were back in that room with those pesky cats. The fluffy ginger one Marie called, Iggypop, hissed at me, but then I saw Alpha. She looked up at me. I sensed that she remembered me. I felt our connection.

Marie put food and water out for me. Later, we watched the TV in that basement room, and Alpha sat on the sofa with Peter and Marie. This routine was much the same as at the house on Pickwick.

That night, I slept on the carpet beside the bed upstairs. The ginger cats both slept on the bed, but Alpha disappeared. *She still does her own thing.*

The next day, Peter drove me out to Alpha Meadows. I knew where I was going as soon as the car turned off the highway and I could hear the crunch of gravel roads. I tapped on the window. Peter reached back and rolled it down. I could smell my terrain. My tongue hung out as the wind blew back my ears. *Alpha Meadows!* I knew it as we slowed down to cross the bumpy rocks of the ford. Up the hill we went, and stronger smells of my kingdom wafted on the air. Past old Sartin's place we drove, where one of my cousins ran out into the road. *He's never been very bright.*

We turned into the drive. We passed Laughing Dragons' Lodge, the orchard, and then turned to the right…there was the house. We stopped by the oval lawn, and Peter let me out. I smelled the grass. *I'm home.*

I explored. The garden was looking good. The grass was all cut, except the oval lawn that Peter started to mow right away. I peed on the big barrels on the terrace that were overflowing with lush plants, just like I remembered. *Oh, bliss!* I drank from the wall-fountain, then wandered back up into the horses' field. It was all mown. As I started to wander toward the big pond, Peter yelled at me, "No, Orbit! No! You're all white. Come back here!" Well, there were no horses and no donkey to chase, so I came back to the oval lawn that smelled of those fresh grass cuttings.

Peter finished mowing and brought me inside the house. He busied himself vacuuming and polishing the furniture. He even covered up old scratches on the doors with a liquid that made them less visible—scratches I had made on some of the wooden panels. I sat on the light-beige carpet, and noticed in contrast that I really did look very white. When Peter set the dinner table, I became more suspicious. I knew this routine. Someone was coming to the house. *Could it be…?* When Peter left all the lights on, and beckoned for me to get in the car, I knew. *Yes, we're going to the airport.*

I slept most the way, but sure enough, we ended up at the airport. Peter left me in the car, and I watched as he walked back across the street to the buildings. It was dark now, and eventually I lay down on the back seat of the Explorer and dozed…

Suddenly, the car door opened. I heard Bettine's voice. "Orbit! Orbit!" she shouted. I jumped out, and rolled on the parking lot tarmac, my legs flailing in the air. "Orbit, you look so white!" Peter was just standing there grinning, with Bettine's suitcase beside him. Bettine knelt down and hugged me. When she stood up, I put my paws on her. "You do remember," she said. "Orby, you do remember me."

How could I ever forget you?

Peter loaded the luggage behind the seats.

"Can I ride on the back seat with Orby?" Bettine asked.

"Of course."

I tried to jump up into the car, but my back legs slipped a little. *It isn't as easy as it used to be.* Bettine helped me, and then sat beside me. I lay down, my head in her lap. Peter drove us home. *Home...Alpha Meadows!*

At the house, it was the old routine. Peter showed Bettine every room. I followed them, even out onto the terrace. The lights from within made large patterns of yellow on the paving stones and illuminated the flowers. The waterfall and the wall-fountain played their magical serenade, and Bettine and Peter hugged each other like old times. "Now, we'll have a little supper," Peter said.

Inside, we returned to the kitchen and dining area. Peter opened the refrigerator and brought out two decorated plates that smelled of fish. "Smoked salmon," he said. He opened a bottle of wine. "Welcome home! It's been almost two years!"

I sat beside Bettine, who gave me a piece of her pink fish.

"Orbit has been doing great work with handicapped children," Peter said. "Nanette takes him to school in Nixa."

Yes, and I get lots of baths. That's why I'm so white.

Peter and Bettine sat at the table, looking across at each other. At times, they held hands. So, I was surprised when Peter got up and said he must go. "Take care of Bettine, Orby. I'll be back for you next week." He left and drove away.

Bettine unpacked some things, turned out all the lights, and we snuggled together on the bed. Later, I went out on the deck. The night air was crisp, but I could see all those stars—*the angels.* Sometimes, I saw them out at Nanette's farm when I lay on the deck with Princess Pony, but I rarely saw them in Springfield. Bettine let me out early the next morning. I circulated my old kingdom, barking for all I was worth.

Peter came back a few days later. Apparently, they were to do the taxes. Taxes had something to do with money, and meant lots of papers on the dining room table. *Money... I don't like money. Money was what caused all that fierce talk here when things started to go wrong.* I got bored as they sat at the table making lists. I pawed at Bettine, and she let me back out on the oval lawn. Taxes done, Peter left, but we saw him again a couple of days later when he came to mow.

Bettine took me into Springfield several times. We visited the Unity church, and I saw Alex, his friend, Emma, and Nadia. Bettine played her flutes at the service. Another time, we visited the people at the printing place. They were so pleased to see me, both the Daves. I inspected the machines, and Bettine left with several boxes of what she calls, product. Then there was the Dub Center place. They all remembered me. But, after visiting the Dub Center, we went back to Marie's. Peter and Marie followed us to my favorite Japanese Restaurant. *They don't let me in there, but Bettine always brings me a box of rice and other good tasting things when she comes back to the car.* When they came out, Peter didn't come back to Alpha Meadows with us, but stayed with Marie in his car. *Bummer!*

A few days later, Peter came back, however. It was in the middle of the night after Bettine had packed her suitcases. *Oh no. She's going away again.* It was still dark all the way to the airport, and Bettine sat beside me. We were both only half-awake.

At the airport, Bettine hugged me on the back seat and whispered, "Be good, Orby. I don't know when I'll be back again, but you know how much I love you." I could feel tears from her cheeks.

Peter drove me to the parking lot. He left, and when he came back, the sky was lightening. We drove back to Marie's. I spent another day with the cats, and Alpha sniffed at me. Perhaps she could smell Alpha Meadows. The next day, the door bell rang. I barked. When Peter opened the door, there was Nanette, and in the drive, my favorite white car. Marie hugged me. Peter ruffled my ears. "I love you, Orby," he said. Soon, I was sitting up in the back seat, even though the day was quite cool. The wind rushed past me, and in minutes I could smell the house on Pickwick.

Nanette didn't take me out to the farm much anymore. In fact, the one time we did go out there, all the furniture was gone. I saw Princess Pony, however, and Pele wanted me to run with him in the meadow, but it was hard now for me to keep up with him. My back legs seemed much stiffer than they used to be. On our return journey to Springfield, while Pele and I sat in the back of the white car, Nanette, explained what was going on. "We won't be going there anymore," she said. "The farm's sold. Someone else will be living there."

What about Princess? I looked at Pele. I knew we both sensed something sad.

Things were different now. Pele came with me to the Nixa school. "I want you to learn from Orbit," Nanette said to him. "Orbit won't be with us all that much longer."

What? What's going on?

A man came to the house a few times. He was dark-looking with wavy black hair. The old woman referred to him as, "the Arab." Nanette often drove away with him in his car. Sometimes, Nanette was away two or three days. Nadia and Alex took Pele and I walking on Pickwick Street. We watched TV, and when it snowed, we all played in the backyard. But, something was definitely different.

The day came when Nanette packed my dog bowls and my blanket in the front of the white car. Alex and Nadia hugged me.

"Jump in Orbit," Nanette said. "We're going to the house on Minota Street."

Why?

After just a short drive, we were back at Marie's place. Nanette gestured for me to get out of the car. We went up the steps to the front door. In no time, Peter and Marie had it open. They both seemed so excited.

"Orbit, you're home," Marie said. Peter was caressing my ears. I could remember way back when Johnny used to caress my ears. Alpha Cat sniffed and walked around me. *Home...another home. Well, at least Peter and Alpha are here.*

Nanette stayed awhile, chatting with Marie over steaming mugs of some warm beverage they called, tea. I wandered into the kitchen, where Marie had put down my water bowl. I started lapping, and soon Alpha was walking under me, rubbing against my legs and mewing.

Nanette and Marie continued chatting excitedly.

"So, how soon are you getting married?" Marie asked.

"As soon as our loft is finished. You must come to our housewarming. You'll love Ahmed."

I stopped drinking and raised my ears. *Ahmed the Arab?*

"He's from Iraq," Nanette explained. "Generally, in Iraq, dogs are not much loved, but Ahmed just loves Orbit. He often says he wishes all dogs could have Orbit and Pele's goodness, but there just isn't room for Pele and Orbit in our tiny loft."

"Well, I don't think the cats will be as much of a problem as we once thought," Peter said. "And Orbit does seem really pleased to see Alpha again."

No room for Pele and me in the loft. Now, it's all making sense.

I settled in pretty quickly at Marie's, but I missed going to the Nixa school. I had got to really enjoy being around children. Sometimes, when Marie and Peter took me walking, children ran up to me, and they always wanted to pet me. Most the people we met were very nice to me. I visited several homes in the area as Marie seemed to know many of our neighbors. "Meet my polar bear," she always said. By now, I was beginning to get curious about polar bears. *Apparently they are white and large, and live up near the North Pole. Well, that's what Marie says.*

An elderly man used to visit Marie's house. He always wore a cap—one of those caps Peter calls, a baseball cap. He used to sit on the sofa in Marie's front room with her, and they would drink tea and eat cookies. He had a funny name—just Beecher. He loved me. Marie introduced me as her polar bear, but Beecher usually called me, Orby, just like Bettine. He would let me sit beside him, and he kept patting me on my head.

As spring began to turn into summer, Peter used to take me out to Alpha Meadows, where he would spend the day mowing, weeding, and watering the flowers. I spent the day wandering around my old haunts, but I didn't run much anymore, except when I saw a rabbit one time while we were all at Laughing Dragons Lodge. Actually, it was during one of Bettine's visits when I was staying out at Alpha Meadows.

Fred and Kiri invited everybody to a barbecue picnic. Sonja, the red-headed lady came, and Josephine Moon, the one who had helped Bettine pack up those things that were taken away from Alpha Meadows in that big truck. Peter and Marie arrived while M and M were cooking chicken and sausages on the grills. I saw this rabbit run out into Fred's field, so off I went, bounding, my ears flying just like in the old days. Of course, the rabbit got away, but I really felt it when I came back. My hips and my back leg joints hurt. I slumped down beside Dick, and lay panting awhile. I hadn't seen Dick for a long time, but I remembered how he used to invite me into his cabin in the woods, and how he would stroke me as I lay beside him. I looked up at him, my tongue hanging out. There weren't many of the others around anymore, but Clive was still there. Holly came with her lady partner, Patti. I had seen their girl, Chancy, before; but Chancy was now much bigger than I remembered her, I think what you humans call, a teenager. M and M's child was there, too, but she was much younger than Chancy. I hadn't seen Kiri for a long time either. She was surprisingly nice to me, although I still wasn't allowed inside the house. *Well, same old same old.*

I looked at Fred when Kiri shooed me out of the kitchen. He seemed a lot less active these days. I remembered how he used to ride motorcycles through his woods. In those days, even Kiri started to ride a bike. But these days, Fred just sat in a chair with a benign smile on his face and a floppy straw hat on his head. He seemed thinner than I remembered him. Everybody made a big fuss of him. *Something's not right here.* M and M served him his chicken first, but he only ate one piece and pulled apart his second to share with me.

After we had all eaten, Kiri made everyone sit on the steps at the end of the Laughing Dragons' deck. They took photos. I was right in the center on the first step beside Dick and Bettine. I remembered all those pictures that George had taken of me when Bettine was at Alpha Meadows before. I knew how to pose and look right at the camera. Marie moved to the front step, insisting on Peter taking a photo of the whole group while she had her arms around me. *Oh well, whatever she wants.*

When everyone left, I sensed some sort of finality to this gathering. Later, I realized there was. This was the last time I saw my friend Fred. Later, Peter said he was very sick, and that he died. "Cancer," he said.

I spent a lot of time with Peter out at the park, as he called it. The park was a beautiful place; lots of grass and trees, and flower gardens where Peter spent many hours working away, just like he had in the old days at Alpha Meadows. He used to tie my leash to a tree, so I could lie in the shade and watch him. Actually, I never took my eyes off him, other than the odd times that other people's dogs came over to introduce themselves. It seemed to be mostly smaller dogs that were curious to meet me. Whatever, there were lots of dogs in the park—all sizes and breeds. Sometimes, Peter and I stayed out at the park a long time and I would half sleep, always keeping one eye just open enough so I could see Peter. Then back we would go to Marie's house. *I suppose I should really call it my house now.* Every evening, Peter and Marie took me for a walk around the neighborhood. Sometimes, we met Beecher when we were out. When that happened, Marie would stand around talking for ages. I wanted to get on with marking my trees and posts, and check who else had been out that day. There were several other dogs that walked in our neighborhood.

One evening, when we came back from the park, Marie was waiting for us on the front porch.

"Your sister called," she said, urgently. "Call her back. It's about your Dad."

"My father?"

"Yes! He's in the hospital. You need to call her right away."

Hospital?

After that, there was a lot of serious talk, and I picked up that Peter might have to go to England. Sure enough, two days later, he left.

Marie and I were alone. I wasn't sure why Peter had to suddenly leave us, and at first, I was somewhat stubborn when Marie tried to take me out on walks. It wasn't going to be the same without Peter. After she put the leash on me, I would sit on my haunches and refuse to get up. But, when you have to go, you have to go. I could hold my bladder a long time, but eventually, I had to let her take me out.

We walked longer than usual, and paused for Marie to speak to one or two people. Marie was more patient with me than Peter, though. She stopped at every tree to let me pee. Over the next two weeks, we really bonded. Walking with her was more like walking with Nadia. Of course, I remembered how I would walk everywhere with Peter in those days when I ran free at Alpha Meadows. I was never on a leash. Now, however, I grew to really look forward to the moment when Marie would pick up my leash and let me know we were going for a walk. Sometimes, Alpha escaped when Marie opened the front door. Marie used to worry about that, but when we came back, Alpha was always up on the porch waiting to come in. It reminded me of early mornings at Alpha Meadows. When

Peter or Bettine let me out at first light, Alpha was usually waiting to come in, sitting outside the sliding-glass door. Peter used to say, "Orbit out! Alpha in!" At night, Alpha used to go out about the same time as I would ask to go on the deck off the bedroom, usually about an hour after Peter and Bettine came to bed. I don't know what Alpha did all night, but she was always ready to come in when I would go outside at dawn.

Peter was away quite a long time. Marie said his father died. *Like Fred and Ninja.* But, while Peter was gone, there was a fierce thunderstorm. I never did get used to thunderstorms, even though they were quite frequent, especially this time of the year—late spring. With Peter being away, the night I started to hear that first rumble, and I seemed to hear it before Marie, I moved from the new, sheepskin pet blanket Marie had bought for me and placed on Peter's side of the bed, and curled myself up as close as I could on the rug at Marie's side of the bed. With the next crash of thunder, I pawed at the bedding. I would have liked to have got up on the bed, but those ginger cats wouldn't have let me. They wouldn't even let Alpha on the bed; she still slept downstairs on Peter's sofa. Marie stroked my head. "It's all right Orbit. It's just a storm," she said, but I still shivered when I heard the noise. I remembered how I used to snuggle up to Alex on his bed when it stormed.

During this time, I became very close to Marie. I wanted to protect her. I sensed she needed me. I followed her around the house wherever she went. She said, "You are my shadow." Even when Peter came back, I didn't want to go for walks in the neighborhood unless Marie came with us. Peter was away most the daytime, anyway. He got up early to drive to Branson, and he didn't get home until it was almost dark.

About three weeks after he came back from England, however, he stopped going to Branson. He seemed worried. "Orbit, I need to get another job," he said. But the good thing was that he took me out to the park a lot that summer. I would watch him as he worked in the gardens. Many people got to know me.

Summer lingered through to October, but when winter came, we spent less time out at the park. I got used to Marie's mother and father coming around to our house. They brought food for the cats. That fluffy ginger cat, Iggypop, still hissed at me. Then, the suitcases came out. *Is Peter going away again? Am I going to be left with Marie?*

Marie kept asking Peter about clothes and shoes. "What do you think of this?" she asked.

"Perfect."

She held up a skirt. "Don't you think my boots would go better with that? I think that's what I should wear on the plane."

"Okay, that will also look great."

She held up another woolen plaid skirt. "I think this would be better."

And so it went on. *She must be going, too. Where am I going to go? Nanette's? Maybe I'm going to visit Pele for a while? I wonder if Pele is still going to the Nixa school?*

The ginger cats seemed somewhat annoyed that the big bed where they liked to sleep was covered in clothes.

"It'll be cold in Scotland," Peter said. "Take both those long woolen skirts."

Scotland? Where's that?

In the middle of all this, a thin, gray cat took up residence on our porch. I felt a little sorry for him. He mewed whenever I went out with Peter and Marie to walk. He had a beaten-up ear and seemed a rather lost character. At first, Marie called him, Mr. Crumple. She wrapped him in a blanket and tried to feed him.

Marie's mother came by. She smiled when she saw Mr. Crumple.

"If he stays, can you see he gets food, too?" Marie asked.

"That'll only make him stay."

Later that same day, Peter and Marie gathered up my bowls, and we went for a short ride in the car. We stopped at a house on the corner of two streets. There was a fence around the back yard. Marie's mother came out. Peter attached my leash, and we went up steps into the house, Marie carrying my bowls. Immediately, there was fierce barking. I noticed several cats, too. They rose on their haunches when I came in and arched their backs. I recognized Marie's father. But it was this small dog with tufty ears and unruly hair that fell over his eyes, who was making most the noise.

"Quiet, Tazman!" Marie's father said. "Orbit's a good ol'e boy."

Well, I guess this is where I'm going to stay.

I flopped down on the soft carpet, while the Tazman dog growled.

The cats settled down on two big sofas, but their eyes were firmly beamed on me. I heard the word "Scotland" again.

"See you at nine for the airport," Peter said to Marie's father.

They left. I was alone in a new house with a yapping dog. I needed to stake out territory. I decided that my spot should be just off this room with the cats and Tazman. It was an area that looked like it guarded the real entrance to the house. *Well, that's my task now, to guard this house.*

The days went slowly in my new environment. Marie's mother let me outside early to pee in the fenced yard before she left every day. My mornings were peaceful, shared with the sleeping cats. The Tazman didn't join us until Marie's father appeared about the middle of the day. Then we all went out in the fenced yard together, although the Tazman didn't pay much attention to me. This was a little different from Pele, Robin Hood, and Little Jon, but then, they were more my size.

Back inside, the big TV screen was on all day, and that actually helped pass the time until Marie's mother came home in the evening, and immediately filled my food and water bowls in the kitchen.

Marie's father used to stay up a good part of the night, sitting at his computer in a little room off the area I had staked out as mine. This made me feel I had a purpose. *My task is to see that the cats don't pass me to disturb him and the Tazman.* And so I lay there, and if one of the cats approached, I just reached out with my paw. It was enough. They soon learned. *They're easier to control than Iggypop and Ringo, those ginger cats at the house on Minota Street.* When Marie's father finally left the little room to go to bed, he would stand looking at me, and he always said the same thing, "You're a good ol'e boy, Orbit." It was a pretty fixed routine, but I wondered if I would ever be able to roam freely again like at Nanette's farm or Alpha Meadows.

It was quite late one evening. Marie's father had been out in his truck. Not too long after he got back, there was a knock on the back door. The Tazman started to bark. I raised my ears. It was pretty unusual for visitors to come by this late. When Marie's father opened the door, there was Peter. I barked with surprise.

"Orby!" he said. "I hope you've been good."

"He's been easy," Marie's father answered. "He's no trouble. Orbit's a good ol'e boy."

I went up to Peter and sniffed at him. He rubbed my ears.

Marie's mother came out from the back of the house. "How was Scotland?"

Scotland? There it is again. Where is this Scotland?

They didn't talk long, however. Peter picked up my bowls, and soon we were in his car.

When we got back to Marie's, despite the cold night air, she was sitting on the front porch with Mr. Crumple in her arms.

The gray cat's still around.

"I guess he's ours now," Marie said to Peter. "He must have stayed close by all the time we were in Scotland."

Mr. Crumple. Now, there will be four of them. At first, however, I felt quite sorry for Mr. Crumple. His beaten-up ear reminded me of poor Harry Trotter's ear after I had savaged it. I suppose that's why Marie called him Mr. Crumple. I have never forgotten what I did to Harry. The pig seemed to forgive me, and he really was a very happy animal. I can see his little tail frantically moving from side to side. I should never have hurt him. I regret ever hurting anyone. In many ways, it was Harry who taught me to love everyone. Now, Mr. Crumple was the new animal at our house. *He's going to have to get acclimatized to Iggypop and Ringo, and the still fiercely independent Alpha. I must be kind to him.* Iggypop just hissed away at him, like she did to everybody. *Well, I'm home again.*

That tree, with all the lights, was put up in the front room. Marie said, "It is my tree of hope and light." Parcels in colored paper appeared beneath it, and Iggypop sat under the tree, pulling at the lowest branches as if she was trying to eat them. Outside it snowed. *It must be Christmas.* I noticed how Ringo's face lit up. The tree seemed to have a mesmerizing effect on both the ginger cats. Alpha Cat, however, didn't pay much attention to it. She spent more of her time on the sofa downstairs.

When Christmas came, it was the usual story—lots of paper from the parcels all over the floor, the cats chasing invisible mice among the rippage; summer sausage for me; lots of tins of Fancy Feast for them. Peter and Marie sat around in their robes, and drank a funny, cream-colored drink in their crystal glasses. Eggnog, they called it. *I wonder where all this Christmas stuff comes from?*

Peter and Marie took me out walking in the snow. One of our neighbors had an inflatable snow person in his yard. I was reminded of the blow-up snow people and that funny man in a red cap and red coat, who had glasses perched on the end of his nose, that Brendan and Rhoda used to put up at our guesthouse at Christmas. According to Peter, they all burned in the shed when we had that fire out there. *No matter, I didn't like them very much, but they must have had something to do with Christmas.*

On our walks in the snow, whenever we met other people and their dogs, Marie always introduced me as her "Polar Bear." It reminded me of something. At Alpha Meadows, apart from those fake penguins that Alpha tore up, there were lots of bears—not real bears—stuffed bears, but Peter and Bettine were always pretending they were real, and would make them talk. Sometimes, they made them talk to me. These bears sat around the house in family groups. Now, some of them were sitting around in Marie's house. There were the teddy bears, the white bears, the panda bears, and the backpacks. *I suppose the white bears are the polar bears.* The head of these backpacks, however, was a very pompous bear, who traveled a lot with Bettine. In fact, it was through Bettine making this overbearing creature speak to me that I learned about some of the places she visited when they went away on those long concert tours. His name was just, Bacpac. He had a companion, who was a gray bear with a very flat face, strange-looking ears, and sleepy eyes. I remember one morning, Peter animating this bear. I was lying on the floor in front of the log fire in the great-room at Alpha Meadows. Peter and the bear approached. Peter, in a voice that twanged a little bit like Arlo's, the Australian who had done so much of the work on the fencing and terrace at Alpha Meadows, made the bear say, "Hi, Orbit. People think I'm a bear, but I'm not a bear, I'm a marsupial." I have no idea what a marsupial is, but thinking back on this incident makes me sometimes want to say to Marie's friends, "I'm not a polar bear, I'm a Great Pyrenees."

It was no better in the summer out at the park. When I was walking with Peter, children often came up to pet me, and called me a polar bear.

That summer in the park, there was a lot of construction going on.

Peter said they were building a Botanical Center. I don't know what that means, but in time I came to know that building very well.

One day, when Peter took me to the park, I knew something was different. Peter was wearing what he called, a cowboy hat and boots that I hadn't seen him in before. These were not his usual park clothes. When I jumped down from the back seat of the car, I heard music. It was coming from under trees, and when we got closer, I could see that lots of people were sitting around on chairs in the shade. Musicians, fiddlers, and singers were performing. There were some other dogs, sitting with their owners, and as Peter and I walked around, I could sense that we were being much admired.

"Like the hat!" a man called out.

"Well, I never get to wear it," Peter said. "Blossoms and Blues seems the right occasion."

"Blossoms and Blues?" So, that's why all these people are here?

A little dog sniffed at me, and I put my head down close to his. I think he got scared, because he jumped back and barked at me—a rather high-pitched bark, not deep like mine. A lot of the people then looked around at me.

"What kind of a dog is he?" several of them asked.

"A Great Pyrenees," Peter explained.

"He looks like a polar bear," a little girl chimed in. "Can I pet him?"

And so it started. While the fiddlers played, many children came up and petted me, and several more of them said, "He looks just like a polar bear."

After about an hour, Marie joined us. She was wearing a pretty, green dress, and the sun that played through the trees caught her long, blonde hair. She took my leash and walked me around, while Peter listened to the music. I wasn't so taken with this music. I preferred it when Bettine played her flutes, but I do remember Dick used to listen to this kind of music when I would visit his cabin at the community. He used to call it, Ozark music. *"Blossoms and Blues"—that seems to be what they call it here.*

Of course, Marie continued to introduce me to everyone as her "polar bear." *I guess I just have to get used to this.* Some people laughed, but most just petted me, rubbing my ears, and patting me on my head and shoulders. When we came back to Peter, for just a moment, on hearing a high note from the fiddle, I looked at the musicians and let out a short, high howl.

"He sings," Marie said to some stranger, who just smiled.

I can sing better than that. I sat down and eyeballed a good-looking, lady Labrador.

Not long after the Botanical Center building was finished, there was an even bigger concert on the lawn. When Marie brought me to this concert, Peter was on stage, talking to all the people seated on the grass. By now, many people at the park knew me by name. Apparently, the concert was being performed by some singer Peter announced as Judy Collins. Marie didn't like to be in the sun, so she found a place under trees on the side of the Great Lawn. I sat there, and many dogs, walking with their owners, stopped to check me out. I was bigger than most of them, but not all. A Great Dane came by.

The music drifted in and out as we were quite a long way from the stage. In fact, it was very strange, because other music was coming from across the lake. It was a bit confusing. I became more interested in a large vehicle parked in the middle of the Great Lawn that made a bucket go up and down, taking people high above us. *Why are they going up there?* I wanted to go over and investigate, but Marie had control of my rather short leash. So, I settled down to watching the small, buzzing insects in the grass.

It wasn't long after that, we left and went home, but I saw that Great Dane several times when Peter brought me out to the park. Park days became less frequent now, though, as winter was coming and the weather was much cooler. I knew we must be getting close to Christmas again, because Peter put up that tree with the lights, and Marie hung many small objects on the branches. *Oh yes...the snow people time.*

Then the day came that made me realize why Marie called me a polar bear. I was a polar bear...Peter's polar bear. I went with Peter to the Botanical Center building. I wasn't usually allowed inside. This day, however, I stayed there all day. Peter dressed up in a bulky white outfit with gold baubles around it, and a funny hat. His face looked more like mine, covered in white fur, and he was wearing big, black boots. He sat in a large chair covered in sheets, and had a big sack of things beside him.

"Now Orby, sit here," he said, after he had taken off my leash. "Now, you really are a polar bear...Kris Kringle's polar bear."

Who's Kris Kringle? Most the people there called Peter, the White Santa.

There were other strange people with us in the big entrance area of the Botanical Center. Someone, dressed up like Marie's tree of hope and light, was reading to kids from a big book. Another human was dressed up like a brown animal with a protruding, red nose. They called him, Rudolph, but all he did was wave his arms around. Finally, there was a snow person. I liked this snow person a lot more than those blow-up people that glowed. They called him, Frosty, and he sang songs. Two others were dressed in green and red outfits and wore pointed hats and curly shoes. But, you know what...more people came to see me than any of these strange people. *It must be pretty important to be Santa's polar bear.* So, all day I let people pet me—girls and boys, and even babies. They all came to us so they could visit Peter, sitting on his lap, and then putting their hands in the big sack of goodies. No sooner had they got their goodies, and they slid off his lap and came to pet me. I stayed there all day. I just lay there, looking at the kids, and letting them stroke me and talk to me, except when one of the funny green and red people took me outside to pee. Those people were apparently elves. You remember, I told you I would tell you about elves. They are Santa's helpers, kind of jolly, and they remind me of Johnny with his mischievous sparkling eyes when I was just a puppy.

"Is it cold at the North Pole?" one of the children whispered in my ear.

How do I know?

"Do you live in an ice house?" another asked me.

"An igloo stupid?" the kid's sister said.

What's an igloo? Well, who cares?

I let them play all over me, just as I had been trained to do at the Nixa school. Every so often, Peter, or as they said, "Santa," fed me ginger cookies. Then all of a sudden when there were not so many children around, Peter got up from the chair and started dancing with the tree. It reminded me of those times when Peter would dance on the terrace with Bettine. I wanted to join in, and I went up to Peter and tapped him with my paw. "Orby loves to dance," Peter said, releasing the tree person. He pulled me up and I took a few steps on my hind legs, just like in the old days, but it hurt now. Soon, I had to let go.

It was a long day, and I was very tired when we went home, but now I really knew why so many people called me a polar bear.

CHAPTER FOURTEEN
The Trauma of Old Age

"When a walk becomes both a joy and a challenge."

I REMEMBER THE DAY THAT Peter had to lift me up onto the bed. I remember the day that my back legs failed, and I stumbled down the stairs into the basement room at Marie's house. I remember that day when I went out to Alpha Meadows with Peter, and found it really difficult to walk up the hill from the guesthouse. I didn't notice it so much going for walks in Marie's neighborhood. There were no hills to slow me down, but every time we went out to Alpha Meadows, I noticed, more and more, how hard it was becoming for me to run around. I didn't run at Marie's or even at the park, because I was always on a leash, but at Alpha Meadows I had always run around in total freedom. Now, I couldn't. It frustrated me, and I would take it out on Peter by digging myself places to lie down in the flower beds or in the gravel near the front door. Peter didn't like this. "Look, Orbit, you're covered in dirt," he would say, "and don't dig holes in the flower beds!" *I'm a self-cleaning rug,* I wanted to tell him. And it was true. Mud would dry on me, and then just fall off my coat. It always had, even after I had stood among the water lilies in the horses' pond.

Peter took me to Aunt Ellen's in Fordland for a bath and trim. *Bettine must be coming home.* He had to stay and help Aunt Ellen get me in the tub, because my back legs were giving way on the boards. "You can do it, Orby," he said, holding my buttocks up, while my front paws tried to grip the slope. I slipped backwards. Peter caught me. And up the perilous slope we went again. This time, I made it. I jumped into the soapy water. "Well done, Orby! Good doggie!" Peter said, before slipping away and leaving me to Aunt Ellen's treatment. The warm, soapy water now felt good, and when Aunt Ellen scrubbed my back, I could feel a tingling down my spine.

Bettine only visited now about once a year, and usually only for two weeks, but when Peter took me to the airport, I felt the excitement of our reunion. I always stayed with her when she was at Alpha Meadows. There, every morning, I went outside and barked around my kingdom, just as in the old days, but I didn't run. I just couldn't run any more.

About this time, a small lump that I had always had on my tummy got bigger, and I licked at it a lot. The skin got raw around it. Eventually, Peter took me to Dr. Espey. I never minded going there, because there were usually other dogs waiting their turn. We greeted each other and wagged our tails. Dr. Espey wasn't too concerned about my lump. "It's just fatty tissue," he said. "But he does have another one on his neck."

Peter felt my neck. "Is that serious?"

"Oh no, it's just the same as the one on his belly. Old age! I'm much more concerned about his hips. They're getting worse. I recommend we give him an injection once a month. It will delay the process somewhat, but it's just old age."

*Old age...*I looked knowingly up at Dr. Espey.

He patted my head. "You're just getting older, Orbit. I'm going to give you some tablets, too. They'll give you more daily comfort."

And so a routine started—a pill first thing every morning, and a trip in the car to Diggins once a month to have a needle stuck in my butt. Then, like on those pesky cats, once a month, Peter squeezed a little tube of liquid onto the back of my neck. He had done that from time to time throughout my life. "For fleas and ticks," he said. "With all these cats there might be fleas."

Well, after all, Mr. Crumple had taken up permanent residence with us now. *Perhaps he has fleas or ticks? His name is confusing, though, because sometimes Marie and Peter call him Mr. Crumple and sometimes Mr. Cuddly.* Among the other cats, Alpha was still the escape artist. She often got out when people opened our front door. Sometimes, she'd escape when I went out for my walks. She liked to walk with me, except she was never on a leash. I was pleased when she did. It was a link with our long past, when we roamed freely at Alpha Meadows.

One spring night, I lay on my sheepskin bed. It was always beside Marie's high bed, up onto which I could no longer jump. Ringo, Mr. Cuddly, and Alpha, usually slept now on Marie's bed. Iggypop preferred to sleep in the warm on the top of the heater in the back room. This particular night, Marie seemed to be making a big fuss over Ringo. I hadn't seen much of him all day, but I sensed sadness in the room. Once in a while, Marie carried Ringo around wrapped in a towel. Most the time, the cat was on the bed with Marie. Peter mentioned Ringo's name many times during the night, and Marie left the night light on beside the bed. I couldn't sleep, because I had a strong sense that Ringo was about to leave us. I was right. I heard Marie quietly say, "He's gone." She burst into tears. They wrapped Ringo up in a blanket and put him in his little traveling house. The next morning, I watched from the back room windows when they carried him out in the sunlight and buried him in the garden.

Ringo...gone...gone where? I thought of Ninja, and how Robert had picked up her body when I had shown him where she'd been shot in the woods across from Alpha Meadows. *But no-one shot Ringo. He just died in Marie's arms. I wonder where he is now? Will I die like Ringo? Will I die in Peter's arms? Has that got something to do with "just getting old?"* I remained very quiet that day, as did Marie and Peter. Then I thought of Bettine. *I want to see Bettine again before I die.*

Soon, it was summer. One morning, Peter took me to the park to a wonderful event they called, "Bark in the Park." Dogs of every size and breed were barking and yapping. It looked as if this event was going to be fun. Peter had me on a leash, and we walked on the grass down to where all these tents surrounded the dogs. I knew I was being admired by the other dog owners once we got among them. Of course, some wanted to know what breed I was, but others simply asked, knowingly, "Is he a Great Pyrenees?"

At some of the tents, people gave us bonios and cookies that crumbled in my mouth, leaving tiny morsels on the fur around my jaw's lips. I licked at them with my tongue. At one tent, Peter let a pretty girl lay her hands on my spine. "You can bring him in," she said. "We have had a lot of success with chiropractic on dogs." *Chiropractic?* "I can feel a good flow of energy in Orbit's spine," she continued. I felt a tingling sensation down my back. I liked it. The girl then stepped back. "He's a magnificent dog." *Me, magnificent...*I looked up at her, adoringly, and then at Peter, proudly.

An announcement was made. All the dogs and their owners started to leave the tented area to walk around the lake at the park. I remembered how Peter and I used to walk around the lake, but I knew that would be too far for me now.

"We'll just go a little way," Peter said.

I walked beside a terrier, and a poodle which looked like Pele. Our leashes crossed as we paraded down the narrow path, but we didn't snap at each other. We knew that this was a time to show off our cooperation among our many different breeds.

When we reached the path by the lake, Peter took me over to the tree where I usually sat while he worked in his special garden—his English Garden. "Rest a while," he said. I flopped down. "We'll join them on the way back."

Most the dogs walked all the way round the lake. Peter pulled some weeds, while I watched and waited. When the dogs came back, we rejoined them and made our way up the grass back to the tented area. This time, I walked with a dog even bigger than me—that Great Dane. As soon as we smelled each other, I recognized him as the Great Dane I had met at that "Blossoms and Blues" music festival and on other occasions in the park.

"I often see your dog," the man walking him said.

"Yes, Orbit's well-known in the park," Peter answered. "But he's getting old now. He's in his fourteenth year. That's one hell of an age for a big dog."

"I know. James here is only ten, but that's getting on for a Great Dane. The big breeds don't usually live that long."

Suddenly, I felt sad, even though I was elated to be among so many dogs. I couldn't help thinking of Ringo. *The day will come. One day, it'll be my turn. Where do we go?* But, back at the tents, it was time for treats again.

I went to "Bark in the Park" twice. The second year, I didn't walk in the parade at all. I got scared in the park that summer. Peter took me down to the English Garden one evening, but on the way back to the Botanical Center, my legs gave way, and I couldn't walk. I lay on the path, Peter holding on to my leash. Peter pleaded, "Orbit, it's not much farther."

I could see our car parked just at the end of the path, but I couldn't move my back legs. Peter tried to stand me up, but I flopped back down. People gathered around us. Someone offered me water, squirting it into my mouth from a bottle. That felt good. This time, when Peter raised my legs, I stumbled forward, my eyes fixed on our white car. We made it! Peter lifted me onto the back seat. I was glad when we got home, and I felt stronger when I ate my senior dog mix. *Senior...Yes, I'm now a senior.*

Peter took me out to Alpha Meadows only occasionally now. But after such a visit, I had a really scary experience. I imagine Peter did, too. We'd spent the day as usual, Peter mowing and watering, and for the most part, me laying out on the oval lawn in the shadow of the house. On the way home, just about the time that I would settle down to sleep, knowing that we had left the area, Peter swerved the car. "What the hell was that?" he shouted, as the car started to zig-zag down the hill to the sound of flying gravel. "A bloody car door in the middle of the road!" We were not going very fast, but I knew we were out of control. With a deep thud, the car ran into the roadside bank at a crazy angle. On impact, I fell into the area between the back seat and the front where Peter sat. He tried to open his door, but he couldn't, so he climbed out of the door on the other side. He came round to let me out, but it hurt if I tried to move. There was no strength in my back legs to get me out of the hollow. I was stuck, scared, and whimpering.

A truck stopped, and the driver got out. "I saw, you swerve," he said. "That old door must have fallen off the back of someone's pick-up. It wasn't there earlier. We live right here."

A woman joined him. "Are you all right?"

"I'm fine," Peter said, "but I'm worried about my dog. He can't get out."

"You've cut your hand?" the woman said. "Let me get a damp cloth for you."

The man peered in at me. I was scared, so I barked at him. He jumped back.

"Doesn't look like there's much vehicle damage," the man said to Peter. "Let me see if I can pull your car out."

I heard the clunking of chains, and at first slowly, and then with a jerk and a great clunk, the car moved from the bank and landed back on the road. I yelped.

"Looks like it's only a fender-bender," Peter said, after walking around the car. "Let me see if she can drive."

He started the car. I felt a little more comfortable, even if still wedged between the seats. At least, we were on the level. Peter drove a short distance, then stopped. The woman came back with a clean, wet facecloth, and Peter washed the oozing blood from his hand. "Thanks, it's nothing," he said. "I need to get my dog to the vet in Diggins."

"Check your radiator," the truck driver said. "I think it's leaking. There's water on the road. You may have to top it off." He got something from the cab of his truck. "Here, take this bottle. Top off your radiator down by the ford."

We did so. Then in no time we reached Dr. Espey's place. Dr. Espey came out with one of his assistants, the one who looked a bit like Maryloulena. *I wonder where she went—she, Leone, Arlo, and Gabriel?* Dr. Espey tried to help me out of the car. I hurt, and snapped at him. I didn't want to bite him, but I did want him to know that I hurt.

"Get a muzzle," Dr. Espey said.

When the girl came back, Dr. Espey, his hands wrapped in a towel, slowly eased the muzzle over my head and snout. "Good dog Orbit," he said, and I felt somewhat comforted. Dr. Espey eased me up, and at last I was able to step out of the car.

Inside, they took off the muzzle and started to prod me. Nothing really hurt now that I was standing up again.

"Is he all right?" Peter asked.

"Orbit's fine," Dr. Espey said, and he gave me a bonio treat.

Back at the car, Peter saw water was still leaking. He asked the vet's assistant if she could fill the water bottle up for him. And thus, stopping two or three times along the way to top off the water, we slowly drove all the way back to Springfield and Marie's house. I was feeling just fine again. *Well, now I have something to tell Alpha.* And that evening, Alpha escaped and joined us on our walk down to the end of the street and back.

Bettine came again that summer. It was the last time I went out to Alpha Meadows. I spent nights on the deck upstairs, looking up at that myriad of stars. Bettine had to help me up the stairs, walking behind me, and making sure I didn't slip backwards. In the morning, she would let me out as she always had, so I could rule my kingdom. I couldn't run around the property, but I barked enough to let everyone know I was back, not that I knew anymore who everyone was. Different people were living at M and M's place now. They had a little boy, and from my spot on the oval lawn I could see him walking with his mother. I thought of Gabriel and Maryloulena as I saw these young strangers making their way toward Laughing Dragons Lodge. Then that tune from Unity Church resounded in my head: "*I am walking in the light, in the light, in the light; I am walking in the light, in the light of God.*"

God. What is God? God must be light.

Bettine and I shared a very happy time together that week. We ate steak and chicken cooked on the terrace grill, and George came to visit one night.

"I know this animal hospital in Springfield where they do chiropractic," he said after seeing me drag my hind leg. "It really might help him."

I always liked George. He was kind to me. *Chiropractic...isn't that what they did for me at the dog day in the park?*

Two days later, Bettine took me to that place. When a girl came out to see me, I instantly knew she was the same girl from "Bark in the Park." "Don't I know you?" she said.

"I don't think so," Bettine answered for me. "Orbit's never been here, but I think it might help him. I just want him to be free of any pain. I don't want him to suffer."

I sniffed at the girl's pants. *Oh yes...I know this girl.*

Once again, I felt the wonderful tingling feeling as the girl gently touched me all the way down my spine. Bettine saw that it made me feel good.

Every morning while Bettine was at Alpha Meadows, before I would go out, I sat at the top of the stairs. I wouldn't go down until Bettine touched my back, and that same tingling feeling ran all down my spine. Like the girl at the animal hospital, Bettine had such healing hands.

Holly, Patti, and Chancy, came to dinner another evening. The terrace was still a magical place with the merging sounds of the wall-fountain and the waterfall. There was laughter. It felt like old times.

The next week, we went to Springfield several times, meeting up with Peter and Marie, and a piano player, Harry Beckett. For me, this meant rice and tasty morsels of Japanese food, but apparently it was all about a concert Bettine and Harry were to play together.

"Let's go over to the church and scout it out," Harry said.

It wasn't the Unity church, though. We went to some place where I had never been before. They called it, the Episcopal church. They let me in. The hall was quite dark, but there was a big piano, like the Steinway we had for so long at Alpha Meadows. I thought of the Piano Princess. *Now, she really made the Steinway sound good.* Harry sat at this piano and played something. *He sounds pretty good, too.* So, he had my approval to play with Bettine. Bettine had played a concert at the Botanical Center the year before. I went to that concert with Marie. We sat right up at the front. I could look up at Bettine the whole time. I even thought I might sing, but it didn't happen. In this Episcopal church, I sat with Peter at the back. Marie came, but she was with her friend Beecher. Many people came up and talked to me. I recognized a lot of them from the park. Apparently, this concert was being given to help the park. Two girls, in official-looking tee shirts, seemed particularly to like me. "What's his name?" the older-looking one asked, shaking back her hair.

"Orbit."

"Orbit," the younger one repeated. "That's a funny name."

There was a party in the garden after the concert. The girls introduced me to some of their friends. "Orbit! Orbit! Orbit!" I heard them all call my name every time they came up to me. They had on the same maroon tee shirts that read "Conservatory of the Ozarks." I let them pet me, but I didn't want to stand up. I just rolled over on my back and looked up at them. *I'm getting tired. I want to go home.*

I slept all the way, while Bettine drove us back to Alpha Meadows. At the house, we shared a piece of cold chicken. Bettine poured herself a glass of wine. We went out on the deck and looked over our land luminated by the moon. Back inside, Bettine helped me up the stairs and lifted me onto the bed. We lay there together. Bettine had her arms around me. I slept, but when I awoke, I could hear her breathing near my ear. I sighed with satisfaction.

Peter visited us at Alpha Meadows the next day. The papers were all over the dinner table again, and I heard that word, "Taxes." Later, Peter and Bettine cooked steaks on the terrace, and when it was dark they danced to the music of the French lady—I actually remembered her name— Francoise Hardy. But, the next time he came, it was to take us to the airport. I didn't get out of the car. I just knew that I was never going to see my beloved Bettine again. She hugged me. She was crying. "Goodbye, Orby. You're such a good doggie," she said. I watched as she made her way through the terminal doors. She looked back once, waved, and then she was gone. I could hear Peter snuffling as he, too, held back tears. He drove the car into the parking lot, then, leaving me, walked back to the airport terminal. He was gone a long time, but when he returned, we didn't drive back to Alpha Meadows. We went to Marie's house.

I pretty much stayed at Marie's house after that. One day, Peter came home all excited. "It's happened! Finally, it's happened!" he said. "I didn't think it was ever going to happen."

What?

Marie came out of her bedroom.

"Alpha Meadows has sold, and just in the nick of time. Bettine and I could never have taken it through this coming winter. We were about to go into this dreadful deal with no money down and no guarantees, and then this man from out of state came to see the property. He loves it, and it's a cash deal…the only cash offer we've had in six years!"

Alpha Meadows sold…My home. I looked up at Peter with pleading eyes, but I am not sure he understood.

A few weeks later, I made one last visit to the park. It was cold and wintry, but one last time, I sat at Peter's feet, while children came to sit on his lap. For the event, "Santa and Friends," he wasn't wearing the white and gold suit this year, but a red suit with white trim, and that same wide, white beard.

"Ho! Ho! Ho!" he said to each child. "And have you been good? What would you like for Christmas?"

One little girl said she would like a baby brother for Christmas. I watched Peter think for a moment, and then, with a hand on my head he said, "You know what, everyone gets a baby for Christmas…the baby Jesus." I'm not sure what that means, but I think I saw a smile form on the face of the little girl's mother.

Most the time, however, the children didn't answer, but just looked up at Peter. Peter then got them to look at me. "What do you think of my polar bear?" he would say. Some of them petted me, but most were only interested in all the different candy in Peter's huge, red sack. "Have some of my milk and cookies," Peter said to the children after they helped themselves to the candy, and they slid down from his lap and went to the adjacent table, where plates of cookies were laid out for the taking. *Can the polar bear have some cookies?* Eventually, Peter fed me some.

I was very tired by the end of this day. That evening, after Marie and Peter had gone downstairs to the basement room, I could hear the TV. I dragged myself to the stairs, and took two steps down. My legs gave way. I fell, tumbling and rolling over, landing on my back at the bottom. In the process, I hit a small table and lamp that also fell to the floor in a clatter. I was more scared than hurt, but when I looked up I could see Alpha's ears of concern as she peered over the side of the sofa. *My legs… I just don't seem to be able to use my back legs.* Peter and Marie rushed to my aid, but I didn't want them to touch me. I gathered my strength, and then dragged myself over to my usual spot on the carpet between the sofa and the TV.

Life after that was almost all lying down, sleeping, but with one wary eye on the cats. A new one had come amongst us. They called her, Callie. Callie didn't have much to do with the other three, but spent most of her time crouched up above me on the old sofa in the front room, while I slept on a runner rug.

It was hard to go on my walks that winter. The worst part was just getting off the porch to street level. Marie was very considerate, and I preferred it when *she* had my leash. She always let me sniff at every interesting place along the way. I didn't stop to pee much anymore as it just fell out of me as I walked, leaving a trail along the path. I loved these walks, though. The three of us, sometimes with Alpha following us, would walk slowly half-way down the street, then cross and come back on the other side. People still admired me, but oh… it was an effort. One of my back legs just dragged behind me. But it didn't hurt. *It must be those pills or that jab in my butt, but it really doesn't hurt.*

I didn't like it that I had little control over my bowel movements, though. Marie and Peter were very tolerant with me over this. They just called them, my smellies, and because they were "healthy looking," as Peter said, they didn't make much mess. But I had always known not to poop in the house. Apart from one accident at Alpha Meadows, and it wasn't for lack of trying to tell Peter and Bettine I needed to go, it just never happened. But now, it happened without my even knowing it, at least not until the smell gave it away. It made me feel a little guilty, and I felt ashamed in front of the cats. Those cats always went to their cat box. *Oh, well, old age…*Peter always said, "It's not your fault, Orby, you're a good dog."

Peter lay on the rug beside me and just looked into my eyes. He cuddled up to me. Alpha climbed up on top of him, and all three of us lay together. *Well, I can't get up on the bed or even the sofa anymore.*

Marie started grooming me, combing and brushing out my coat. While she worked on me, piles of my wooly fur gathered on the rug around me.

"You could knit a coat out of that," Peter said.

"He loves it. He's so much easier to groom than Iggypop."

Yes, I've heard Iggypop complain bitterly when Marie tries to get mats out of her fur.

And so it was—a simple routine—a daily ritual that made me comfortable, knowing how much I was loved.

I spent more and more time stretched out in the front room. It became harder and harder to get up. So, Peter and Marie spent a lot of time lying with me.

One day, Peter dropped down beside me with a piece of paper in his hand. "Listen, Orby," he said, "this is a letter for you from Bettine." He started to read, and I could tell it was a passionate letter about my life. At points, Peter even laughed as he read. Then, he came to this part, and he looked deeply into my eyes:

"I thank you with all my heart for being in my life so long—now nearly sixteen years! You are the star of my life and being, and in every show I play now, and forevermore, you are the biggest star, because in my multi-media show from screen and stage you spread your love to millions all over the world. When you go into the other worlds and over the Rainbow Bridge, know that we will always celebrate your continuing presence and life on earth—you were the best thing that came out of that community adventure."

Momentarily, I thought of the child, Gabriel. I could see him at the Unity church, smiling at Maryloulena, while all the other children were singing that song: "We are walking in the light, in the light, in the light; we are walking in the light, in the light of God." *I wonder what it will really be like in these other worlds and over the Rainbow Bridge?*

Peter paused in the reading, as if he knew I was in thought. He patted me on my head to bring back my attention.

"There was a lot of hardship," he continued, reading Bettine's words as he tried not to choke up. "But all the losses and sufferings were worth it just for you. I love you, Orby, with all my heart! I shall miss you, but you will always be in my heart wherever I go, and you will never be forgotten by any being you have known. If a new dog comes into my life, he'll bring me *your* presence. It's all love. All else is illusion. I love you, forever, your human mother, Bettine."

I could tell from Peter's eyes that he was thinking something, and I just instinctively knew what. I remembered those two portraits of that dog by the front door at Alpha Meadows. I knew this dog was special to Peter from some time in his life. I had even heard him speak to the drawings. All he said was, "I love you, Woolly..." He didn't say "I loved you." It was as if for him, Woolly was forever. *Could Woolly also be me?* I put forward my paw and tapped Peter's wrist as he lay beside me.

A few days later, on a morning when I found it particularly hard to stand up, Peter pressed his phone to my ear. I heard Bettine's voice..."Orby, you're such a good doggie…such a good doggie." Then the sound of her flute filled my ears.

"That was Bettine, wasn't it?" Marie said.

"Yes, she played her flute for Orby, one more time."

I knew. We dogs do know. Perhaps humans know, too? *Finality, I know it. My legs have got so much worse. I've fallen many times.* When Peter and Marie tried to hold me up, again I collapsed. They guided me to the rug. I liked it there, and I lay down. I was comfortable, but I couldn't walk.

"Are you thinking what I'm thinking?" Peter said.

"Yes," Marie replied.

Finality. Now I was certain. *Have I made a difference in their lives… the lives of all those humans that I came to know? Did they see my light? Did I spread the light?*

Later, with Peter and Marie holding up my hips, I stumbled out onto the lawn. I sat on the grass in the sun, just as I always had on the oval lawn at Alpha Meadows. It was a beautiful spring day. Marie groomed me, gently caressing my coat with my favorite brush. Peter lay on the grass beside me, looking into my eyes. He held my paw. *I know. It's all right. I know.*

They lifted me into the car. It was only a short drive. They carried me out and set me down in this veterinary office. It was not Dr. Espey's place, but it smelled the same. A chocolate-colored dog came in—a Labrador. He came over to play. He must have been a puppy. I put out my paw for him. I tried to get up, but I couldn't. Two nice girls came out to talk to me. Then they took us into a private place. The girls left. For a long time, Marie groomed me, while I sat with Peter. I could see his eyes were moist. He was stroking me under my chin. *It's all right. It's all right. I'm over fifteen years old. I've had a wonderful life.* At length, the girls came back. They shaved a patch on my back foot, and there was a prick as a needle went in. *I think I have accomplished my goal. I have spread the light.* I felt at peace as I continued to look at Peter, then the room went fuzzy.

EPILOGUE
OVER THE RAINBOW

PETER'S EYE BECAME A MYRIAD of tiny dots…ever smaller, ever more numerous, until it was an eye no more. All I could see was red…millions of red dots. Gradually, the red became orange, then yellow, and then green. I could see these colors far more clearly than I ever had before. The green became blue, then indigo, and finally, violet. It pulsed, and it lightened to pure white.

Humans speak of us dogs "crossing the Rainbow Bridge." Perhaps we do. But they want to relate this Rainbow Bridge to something they always call, heaven. Call it heaven if you like, but it is not a place. I know now. It is all that is.

Oh, I know the human interpretation:

"Just this side of heaven is a place called Rainbow Bridge.

"When an animal dies that has been especially close to someone here, that pet goes to Rainbow Bridge. There are meadows and hills for all of our special friends so they can run and play together. There is plenty of food, water and sunshine, and our friends are warm and comfortable.

"All the animals, who have been ill and old, are restored to health and vigor. Those who were hurt or maimed are made whole and strong again, just as we remember them in our dreams of days and times gone by. The animals are happy and content, except for one small thing; they each miss someone very special to them, who had to be left behind.

"They all run and play together, but the day comes when one of them suddenly stops and looks into the distance. That dog's bright eyes are intent. The dog's eager body quivers. Suddenly, he or she begins to run from the group, flying over the green grass, those doggie legs moving faster and faster.

"You have been spotted, and when you and your special friend finally meet, you cling together in joyous reunion, never to be parted again. The happy kisses rain upon your face; your hands again caress the beloved head, and you look once more into the trusting eyes of your pet, so long gone from your life but never absent from your heart.

"Then, you cross the Rainbow Bridge together."

But when we see the colors of the rainbow eventually pulse into that light that is eternal, we know that heaven is so much more than a place. It is everything that has ever been and ever will be. Once you have crossed the Rainbow Bridge, you know these things on every plane of being.

I am aware of every dog that Johnny, Joanne, Peter, Bettine, Nanette, Marie, and their families have ever known, and they are all a part of me, for now I am aware of all dogs that will be part of their continuing lives, too, and their future families' lives. *Yes, I am in Woolly and Woolly is in me.* I know this now. But I know it without having to reason. It just is. I'm aware of my presence in Penny and Angel. I know you love them, Bettine—two beautiful Retrievers. They share time with you in the meadows and mountains of a faraway land. Their love for you, now that I am no longer experiencing life with you, is the same as my love—it is eternal. What's more, it's not just about dogs. I am aware that everything is connected and that everything lives. I sense only the light, and that must be God. This God is in everything that we encountered on our earthly journey, but now there is no division as to who and what we are. The dog, the human, the cat, the horse, Princess Pony or the Piano Princess—the rocks, the grass, the trees, the river, the clouds—they're all the same. They are pulsating dots of ethereal light, and it is as if they all sing one song in a sound that I can only know, but not hear—the sound of eternal beingness.

I'm aware that there is a marble bench that tells those still living in the illusion of the world that I once lived on Earth. I am aware that it stands in the Springfield Botanical Gardens opposite Peter's English Garden. I am aware that Peter and Bettine buried the dust of my earthly life beside that bench, and scattered some in the garden. I know that Peter still talks to me there. I see you, Peter, every time that you are working in the garden, and I have seen you there, Bettine. I have seen Marie come there. Many strangers have also sat there, inspired by the beauty of the garden—strangers whom I never knew, but I know them now. They have read the inscription you had so lovingly inscribed there…Orbit-In gratitude-Beloved Forever-Bettine-Peter-Marie…and I am in gratitude that you were, my people. Am I there? Of course I am or I would not be aware of all this, but I am equally aware of gaseous swirls that form what you humans call your universe. I am aware that the planet, on which we lived together, is a tiny speck on the outer rim of one of these great gaseous swirls. But, I am also aware that it is not there. I am aware that all those angels in the sky that I once believed to be above Alpha Meadows, what you call stars, were never there, and yet I know they're all there, with many, many more. In the pulsing whiteness, everything is there, and yet nothing is there—nothing that we perceived when we lived the pattern that you call, life. As you wrote, Bettine, in that letter: *It's all love. All else is illusion.*

There is no good, no bad, no rich, no poor, no ugly, no beautiful—only the love of all that is. You strive for it and call it God, but when you, too, cross the Rainbow Bridge, you will be aware of it in the pulsations of white light—you will be one with God, knowing every detail of your universe, past, present, and future. Every small particle of beingness that ever was, or ever will be, is one. I am in you, and you are in me. Over the rainbow there is no separation. Separation is the great illusion.

ACKNOWLEDGEMENTS

I AM GRATEFUL TO PETER Longley and Bettine Clemen Longley for giving me a home and encouraging my philosophical message, and I am also grateful to Nanette Tulak for the very special time I spent with her and her family.

I am grateful to Johnny and Joanne for leading me to Peter and Bettine, and to Marie for taking such good care of me in my later life.

I would like to thank Yakov Smirnoff for the quote I have included in the narrative and on the back cover. He is a very funny, but astute human being. Actually, flattered though I am by his observation, we are *all* spiritual beings.

I also thank Ginny Brancato for allowing me to quote the RainbowsBridge.com version of that anonymous, but much loved poem, *Rainbow Bridge.*

I learned wisdom along the way from many people, animals, and dog friends. Among those people who taught me wisdom, I would include, Johnny, Joanne and Dick from the community at Sarvis Point, Sue Baggett, the lovely lady from Unity Church, Springfield, and Leonard, who loved our apples. I remember affectionately, the Piano Princess and Lori Robinson, who with Bettine, gave me the ability to appreciate music. I remember the kindness of Fred Johanssen, and of Marie, with whom I lived the last years of my life. Most of all, I learned from my people, Peter and Bettine, who shared their lives with me through the good times and the bad, and with whom I will always be connected.

My own brother taught me early wisdom. My mother, Precious, taught me love. Other dogs, who meant much in my life, include, Trail, my first best friend, Bear, who widened my horizons, Ninja, whose life was too short. Pele, who was my protégé, and I also had good times with

Asha, Robin Hood, and Little Jon. Then there was Alpha Cat, with whom I shared much of my life, and other cats, who taught me patience and endurance—Ringo and Mr. Cuddly. There were our horses, Amadeus, and especially Angelo, and at Nanette's farm my favorite, Princess Pony. Of course, there was also Dominique, that funny donkey that taught me that it was all right if people laughed at us, and to turn that laughter into love. Finally, there was Harry Trotter, that potbelly pig. Perhaps he taught me the greatest lesson of all—to be kind to everyone, humans and animals alike. Please forgive me Harry, but I learned so much from the error of my ways. If I had known you earlier, then maybe I would have been kinder to the Amish. We are all united, there is no separation.

The photographs that I have shared with you in this book were taken by Peter Longley and Bettine Clemen Longley, and their good friends Bill Penninger (George), Jackie Warfel, Nadia, and George Freeman. I am grateful for their permission to reproduce them as a companion record to my autobiographical text.

PETER LONGLEY

PETER LONGLEY IS A BRITISH author who has lived in the United States most of his life. Born in Scotland, he was brought up and educated in England, where he gained his masters degree in theology at Cambridge University. He worked for an American family as Estate Manager of Tullamaine Castle in Co. Tipperary, Ireland, from 1966-77, and then moved to Sea Island and St. Simons Island, Georgia, USA. From 1978 to 1997, he was a cruise director with Royal Viking Line and Cunard Line, and traveled all over the world. Today, he works in horticulture as the Horticultural Interpreter at the Springfield Botanical Gardens in Springfield, Missouri.

Peter has several published books including *Two Thousand Years Later (Hovenden Press 1996)* and his award-winning *Love is Where Your Rosemary Grows (iUniverse 2003)*. His definitive work is his trilogy on a plausible life and times of Mary Magdalene. The first book was published as *Legacy of a Star (Durban House 2003),* but subsequently he brought the whole trilogy out in the three volumes: *A Star's Legacy (iUniverse 2009); Beyond the Olive Grove (iUniverse 2009);* and *The Mist of God (iUniverse 2011).* His family memoir and commentary on John Galsworthy's *Forsyte Saga,* depicting the parallel rise and fall of the British upper-middle class and the British Empire, was published as *Forsythia (iUniverse 2012).* Further information on these books can be found at www.PeterLongleyBooks.com or on www.amazon.com

Further information on Bettine Clemen and her music, including Orbit's ability to sing along to her flutes, can be found at www.joyofmusic.com

Printed in the United States
By Bookmasters